Confessional Scriptures

Confessional Scriptures

Biodun Abudu

This is for the sexual folks that took a chance or adventure, and through their journey to find the ultimate satisfaction, have done some things behind closed doors. Just know you are not alone......

Confessional Table of Contents

<u>Writings On The Wall</u>

Confessions

Writings On The Wall

Felon - Breaking Backs

Sex - Plenty

Position - Doggy

Reference - Your mother

Home Sweet Home

He introduced me to his massive dick,
It was big and worth every stroke;
His dick is a ten over ten
and when I sit on it,
There's no place I'd rather be -
because there is no place better than home.

Melt yourself into me and go guts deep

Premium Package

As I salivated and anticipated,
His dick got me at hello;
The size was big enough
It knocked down my walls of Jericho.
32 deep strokes
Is all I needed to become saved,
As he delivered his premium package;
We fucked for 7 days straight,
and on the 7th day my pussy rested.

Rearrange my guts, daddy

A Real Man

I treat my woman with respect
And I handle her with care,
But when I fuck her
I am quite disrespectful,
I am a real man
Who doesn't stop
Till she is satisfied.
I play with her pussy
and not her emotions,
I give her complete satisfaction
At the midnight hour;
So by morning she is a new woman
Who is reborn-with a new pussy
That is hungry all over again;
And of course I'm here to feed it,
Because I am a real man.

Play with my pussy and not my emotions

Filthy Fantasy

So many fine men I can't even pick one,
Line them up, let me suck them- one by one;
Give me different flavors of men,
American, Brazilian, Italian, African and more;
Let one drive by my place on the weekends,
Let another be scheduled to do a live in,
I want one to cuddle with when I feel like it.
Another one to dick me down under the palm trees,
Waking up to someone
eating me out on the beach sand.
Another two can be responsible
for constantly poking my pussy,
Under the moonlight;
With my head on the ground,
and my feet in the clouds,
I'm saying RIP to my pretty pussy
As I pass out from pain and pleasure!

Issa vibe when your dick hits my walls

The Good Life

A fortune cookie once told me
to make sure I get my pussy ate on the regular,
So I made it a mission to cross off my list.
I found a king capable of handling me
When he hits the jackpot-
I start producing lots of juice;
As he slurps
He burps like he's been drinking mimosas.
Feeding him my pussy
like it was a Sunday soul food dish,
He feasts on my pussy and ass like a buffet,
Giving him enough nutrients to supply his whole
generation.
His tongue switches lanes from my pussy to my ass,
He multi tasks with his tongue and fingers,
Leaving my inner temple juicy and wet.
My soul has officially left my body.
As I squirt and he cums,
We both raise a toast to the good life!

Continue eating the pussy until her soul

leaves her body

Honor Thy Pussy

Communication is key-
that's why I need you to talk to my pussy;
Attend to it with respect,
Treat it like it's gold,
Analyze it like it's a dollar bill;
Pamper my pussy!
Kneel before it, worship it,
and shower it with treats;
Make sure all its needs are met.
Use all your resources
From your mouth, hands and down to your dick;
They say paradise is where it's at,
and my pussy is heaven on earth!

Pussy Power

Sex Tape

Sitting on my throne
I look forward to seeing you naked,
Assuming the position on your knees
With your lips on my dick,
Gagging with tears rolling down
So I can record in excitement
And I can zoom in on your pussy!
Admiring how delicate it is-
Being thankful for how pretty it is-
Analyzing how it expands
And mysteriously accommodates my tool
As I ram my dick in your pussy from behind.
Let me violate your body
Choke you and stroke you;
With your pussy and my dick
Being the main characters,
It's always a party central.
Leave your fingerprints on my windows
and let me sign my name on your wet walls.

He was large and in charge

Tap In

Tap into this pussy
And witness
The divine pleasure it brings,
It is a healing factor
With pleasurable pain-
Pain that leaves memories-
Memories that last forever,
Forever that goes on and on
continuously leaving the marble floor wet,
Wet as in waterfalls,
as in the flow of water.
Tap into this pussy
and witness heaven on earth!

Limited Edition Pussy

Midnight Prayers

There is an endless story
in the length of a man's dick,
There is a blessing attached
when it has girth or is thick;
It's hard to explain the joy one feels
Especially when a bitch finds good dick,
You cherish it, pray it never leaves-
and then you pray it hits you in the right angle-
So you don't end up in the hospital.

Paint my tonsils with your cum

Morning Rituals

There's a meeting in my bed,
There are conversations between our bodies;
It's a therapy session with my mouth on your dick.
The morning sun is setting on my pussy,
That's why I need you to get on your knees and
Say your morning prayers in between my legs-
Put your hands together and be thankful.
Insert the necessary fingers needed,
Be appreciative of this marvelous pussy;
Let your mind guide you through my inner walls,
Let your soul be deposited into my temple,
Let your body get familiar with mine,
Prepare yourself for my explosion,
As it may feel like a morning face wash
With my juice dripping from your beard.
This is my gift to you to start your day,
Now go ahead and be great!

Appreciate my pussy

Xpen$ive

Put this pussy away and preserve it
Like an artifact on display,
It's too good to be touched
So admire it from a distance
Because it's expensive,
It's a billion dollar pussy,
Worth tons of euros
Most sought after,
Like a diamond,
Worthy like gold;
Pussy is a part of history-
Pretty, pink and delicate,
It's the passage way
Into this world.
Respect this pussy,
It's the queen mother
That puts you to sleep,
As your eyes roll back and your toes curl,
Give it props and put it in a museum!
Salute it and Worship it
Because it's worth it.

Reckless and offensive

That Special One

I am hoping I will find the one,
Someone that will make it worth living,
and in my times of need
She'll be there with open arms and open legs.
Her presence in my life will be a blessing,
A person that will contribute to my pleasure,
She will play a huge role in my bedroom-
With white sheets, candle lights and music-
As she takes the lead and fucks me so good.

*Everybody wants to eat my ass but nobody
wants to take me out to eat :(*

Sexual Intercourse

Enjoying myself
Feeling nice
Responding to pleasure
From his erect penis
and my humble vagina;
Spasms and Convulsions
Vocalizations and Contractions
Got me feeling like I'm demon possessed
As I scratch his back till he bleeds;
My pleasure and his pain,
What a beautiful way to start the day;
Happy Sunday, he says as he nuts
On my pouted lips!

He's young and healthy in the bedroom

What a Mighty Man

He was a man that was packing for the whole of
Africa,
He rubbed on my booty to calm my anxiety,
He fingered my pussy to release my stress;
Its always a vibe when his big-ass dick hits my
wall.
Every 10 minutes he pulled out to admire my pussy,
He made it his mission to eat me out disrespectful-
ly;
In return, I make sure I suck him with every last
strength,
I will climb mountains and cross seas for his dick-
All because it's worth it.
I'll work a 9 to 5 shift and over time if I have to,
I'll surrender my weekends to him with my legs
wide open,
Trust and believe that this man is worth it!
He is a professional prostate worker with a top tier
dick,
If I died and came back to the world,
I would do him all over again because he is worth it.

He was packing for the whole of Africa

Interlude

You in her DM, I am in her guts,
I am taking this special project
To rearrange her guts;
Painting her tonsils with my cum,
As each drop lands on her face,
She counts 1 sheep, 2 sheep with my cum.

You may need a safe word tonight

Young and Healthy King

I always had a curious tongue-
Hearing him unzip made my heart smile,
It was music to my ears to hear "put it in your
mouth and shut up";
My knee pad was always available to use.
At any given time I was flexible to put my hair in a
bun;
He was my teacher and I was his student-
I was always willing to work overtime.
He was my doctor I was his patient,
He had all special visiting rights in and out of my
body;
He admitted me into his academy
For extra lessons that took my soul away.
He started me out with Vaseline in-between my
cheeks,
As we became closer we transitioned into using
lube;
Then when he wanted to disrespect me, he would
spit;
He never missed and it always landed right on my
hole.

He is my everything, my young and healthy king,
That's why I will always be here to welcome him
With open arms, open mouth and open legs!

Apt 69

If you know me then you would know
That I don't make empty or false promises,
I fulfill all my commitments and duties;
My men always leave my house satisfied;
I open the door naked and on my knees
My knee pads are always ready for use-
When they walk in, they know what to do,
No talking, just unzipping is the motto.
I suck them till they are dry-
Making sure there no single drop left,
Making sure I lick them completely clean!
If they prefer to shoot all over my face
Then my face becomes their canvas;
They shoot their creamy nutrients,
Creating a masterpiece with their thick heavy nut
Dangling from my eye lashes and lips.
Rarely do I swallow or catch,
But if I do- then he must really be worth it!

Hair in a bun and grab your knee pad

Like My Life Depended On It

Kneeling on the concrete floor
With him unzipping his pants,
I look up at his majesty for instructions
He utters no words at all;
He simply points to his thick dick
Like a prayer I closed my eyes,
With my eyes closed and my mouth wide open-
My prayers have been answered!
I moan in excitement
Even though it's a struggle for it to fit.
Spitting on his dick as requested,
Choking him while I ride him,
He reaches higher heights in my tummy-
He rearranges my guts and takes my soul away.
When he explodes, he paints my tonsils;
Looking deep into his eyes
Blowing bubbles with his cum,
Swallowing and thanking him
For providing me a balanced diet,
That I received on my bloody knees
From the concrete floor.

Some throats are just unforgettable

Enigma

I am a mystery that no one can solve
leaving lots of people confused-
a lady in the streets,
but a freak in the bed.
In my leisure time
I grab onto a man's dick
like it was wrapped in cash!
One day I want the president in my bedroom,
Just for the sake of power rubbing on my skin;
The next day I want a thug
That can choke me and slap me around-
A thug that is capable of fucking me till the sun
comes up.
I am an enigma-
Today I may choose to fuck with the lube,
Tomorrow I may grab the Vaseline close to me,
Next week you can just spit and shove it in me;
I am an enigma
And you just cant figure me out.

7 deadly sins and I picked lust and vanity

Nudes

Nudes are precious
and can be quite expensive,
The best thing money can buy
 and worth every penny!
They are visually satisfying-
Hidden in our laptops and phones,
Producing creamy nutrients behind closed doors.
In the comfort of one's home
Nudes are masterpieces,
They are mysteries finally solved,
Once the layers are taken off the skin-
They are powerful
and are the most sought after items
that can either be considered Gold
or the ultimate sin!
It is a visual invitation into one's bedroom,
For a taste of the forbidden fruit;
Nudes are the best things ever created by man.

Nudes are masterpieces

Skin Express

You are his 9 to 5, and I'm his overnight.
You are no longer in his thoughts when I take him
on vacation;
I'm his emergency call when he needs to get his
nut,
He is in paradise when my lips attach themselves to
his dick.
That's why he gives me a weekend call,
Because he knows where the pleasure resides,
You may get him started- but I certainly finish him
off.
I'm his motivation to masturbate,
9 times out of 10 you are tasting my pussy on his
dick.
I am the one clicking reject when you call,
Because he is busy sucking my toes;
My ass and his lips go together,
His dick and my pussy are made for each other.
Whenever, and wherever he is,
He keeps me on his wishlist;
My pussy is the key to his survival!
For that alone you should be thanking my pretty
pussy.

*His dick is big and so is mouth. I am always
orally inspired to take a chance.*

Straight To The Point

When he asks me "wassup?"
I respond with "this fat ass",
It's an open invitation;
And when he comes over-
His basketball shorts
Means easy access!
I place my hand on his lips
So he doesn't talk at all,
It's my responsibility
To take the lead,
Pulling down his pants
And sucking out his nutrients-
It's my duty to relieve his stress
And fulfill his needs.
I don't need his consent to keep riding him,
I am here to help him recognize his potential
till he explodes multiple times;
And when he wakes up
I'll be there to suck him in the morning,
I am the reason he is stress free
Because it's my duty;
Well until someone else calls
Then I'm out!

Sucking out his creamy nutrients

A Great Candidate

I'm leaving behind the Virgin Mary,
And embracing the red scarlet in me;
So skip the hand shakes and pleasantries,
I love a man that looks good
Smells good and fucks good;
I need a man that is hung like a horse!
I need a man that works,
A man that understands the assignment,
A man that puts an icing on my cake
Upon completion;
And because of his skills and hard work-
I'll be giving personal references
To all my friends in need!

He said "Saddle up baby" and I sat on his face

Tour Guide

Let me take your tongue
to places it's never been,
Let me introduce it
to the tastiest things in life;
Let my skin be a map
That your tongue follows to my lady license,
Let it find it's way to my backyard
And create a slurp fountain on my hole;
Let me be able to take you to places
And give you a direct connection
With my pleasure units,
Especially my tropical pussy.

Let me take your tongue to places it's never been

Top Tier Dick

I love my dick
Thick,
Long,
Fat,
Little curved;
Maybe a Captain Hook,
Mostly cut,
Unless he fine as hell-
Then give me an uncut.
Talking about dick
Makes me salivate,
The thought of a dick
Makes me happy from within,
A genuine happiness;
One look at it
and the adventure begins.
It performs magic tricks,
Especially when he is a grower-
So when I see it
I assume the position;
With my wagon waiting for a bruising,
Saying ahh with my mouth
But burping with my ass,
As my pussy is left defeated.

Dickmatized

Triple XXX

I love working from home
So that during my break time
You can shove it down my throat;
Let me gulp your rod hands free,
Then you can flip me over like a rag doll
And eat me out on the kitchen counter
Until tears are rolling down my eyes.
I got a lot of cake-
it could use some dick
So bury my face in the pillows,
and dick me down ruthlessly
Fuck me like your life depends on it
Bust on my face
and bend me over for a part 2
Ram it into my cheeks,
while your cum drips down my face;
Let me be your slut
And your number one fan.

He fucked me so good I was on bed rest to recover. I even needed a wheelchair to move around.

Stone Tablet

Place me on a mountain top
Right beside the stone tablet,
Then devour my pussy under the sunlight
Make your move and set my soul free;
Define what it is to be satisfied
Dick me down under the moonlight,
Place me on a big rock like the Olumo rock
So I can leave my finger prints on them;
Then fuck me inside a hidden cave
So when I scream it echoes,
Then take me to the waterfall
And do my body right, under the water.
Sign your name on the stone tablet
With all of your creamy nutrients,
Let me feel you balls deep in me
So I can give a testimony at the alter-
And at the mention of your name
I know I will always be wet,
Forever reminiscing in my home
With my fingers in between my legs,
Saying to myself "it was the dick" for me.

"Raw is law" he said

In The Closet

I have no desire to compete with pussy
But I want to step in where she lacks,
I am passionate about sucking dick
I have over 10 years of experience.
I'm not a home wrecker
I'm actually there to catch every nut
That he explodes from his thick pipe,
I made a vow to satisfy him,
And whenever he calls for me
I'm one Uber ride away,
Sometimes a flight away,
What we do is understood
We made a vow to keep it in the closet.

Sloppy second & dirty third

Best Kept Secret

The best kept secret in the world is a dick.
Not just a dick, a large thick ass dick-
I'm talking about soda can thick-
One that makes you look in awe,
It leaves your jaw wide open at first sight,
The size intimidates you, sometimes,
Yet you still fall on your knees
Worshipping it!
Despite choking, gagging,
Being teary,
You are still giving your best;
Even when your jaw hurts,
You are still worshiping this masterpiece
Until it responds with a creamy feedback.

When the size intimidates you, just take a deep breath……….

Mr. President

He is the president to the country,
But in my bedroom
He salutes to my vagina;
Soaking his face in this natural spring,
Letting his tongue get familiar with my clitoris,
Then I pull his hair backwards
So he can come up for fresh air.
Nothing too big or small
For me to conquer;
Riding him until the sunrise
As his eyes roll back,
I scratch his back to mark my territory,
He then speaks in tongues
And shoots his nutrients down my throat.

He is my bitch and it's his duty to spread my

pussy lips

Confessions

The Ultimate Sin

In my bed I am tossing and turning with guilt on my chest. The same mouth I use to give advice to my peers and make bold statements that inspire millions is the same mouth I use to satisfy my secret lover. I use my mouth to inspire his dick to move in closer towards my tonsils. I motivate him to grab onto my thighs and ass like his life depended on this great miracle which my pussy supplies. My pussy is a known healer to his stress and other problems.

He is a pastor ! Unfortunately, he is a man of God that splits my thighs apart like the Red Sea and pokes my wall of Jericho. He baptizes me with his creamy nutrients after church services. As I count the offerings and tithes, he is in between my thighs with his head lost in my skirt. I pray forgiveness for I have sinned in the house of the Lord.

I feel guilty- not only because he is a pastor- but because I'm number one despite his marital status. I stay thick, beautiful, looking and smelling like money. He takes care of my every need before I even ask. Every Friday is a pay day and I am woken up with a bank notification on my phone as I roll over to check my phone. He keeps me happy and satisfied. I don't want to let him go, but I know this is very bad. I enjoy seeing his beard soaked in my pussy juice and seeing him gasp for air when I tighten my thighs as his face is in between my legs. I enjoy giving him glorious blow jobs under the church podium on those holy Sunday mornings, he usually gives me feedback when he repeatedly screams hallelujah to the church members. He has learned so much from me, he is my investment.

However I think it's time to let it go, my mother wouldn't be proud of me.

PG 25

My bed is surrounded by velvet ropes and guitars
and with my birthday suit-I'm totally ready for Bed
War 7.

However, I got intimidated when suddenly a halo
floated over his magic stick. I guess I may need an
alteration right before he opens up my golden gates.
The first moment I felt the first attempt I suddenly
started to hear the voice within telling me to exhale.
Maybe I shouldn't have said that all major condoms
were accepted because now my bed mate is about to
pierce me open with a XXXL
magnum.

I already know my next destination is "ouch" sta-
tion, then after I'll be in recovery mode. I finally

met a higher being than the average Joe that runs
out of batteries. This master comes with no batteries
and he seems to be receiving energy straight from
the tight source he is currently exploring.

The facial expressions tell so many stories that
without even talking and sticking to strictly body
language I can tell if I need to switch positions,
bend a certain way or slightly jiggle like I was per-
forming in front of a live audience.

I had half of my face covered with a blind fold. All I
knew was that deadly stunts were in motion, I just
assumed I should go ahead and tell my wet walls
R.I.P., for with that kind of aggression, I doubt it
will look the same. It will be hospitalized for a few
days. It will truly be a sad story- and during my

recovery - I will channel each and every soprano moment.

Murder he wrote, his name definitely will be recorded in the Guinness' Book of Records for the most mentioned name, my bedmate surely works wonders and miracles.

1 Cake 1 Throne

I am your leader, I am the ultimate Svengali, Benjamin Franklin's Bitch and Queen Elizabeth's Bestie. A majestic and edible gift that your mind can gulp at its convenience. I'm the last temptation behind door number three with a body so much like a CL5 that even Pharaoh and Nefertiti numerously tried to test the drive.

Medications prescribed by historical figures couldn't take my presence away. Not even a lame little fellow could cast me away. My empire grows and surpasses my enemies, and along the way I make a quick stop to see their hateful silly faces.

The members of high-class society salute my Egyptian body and in addition to their unwanted service they safe guard my soft skin closely with their eyes.

All that seduction I put on display is for a meaningful purpose. Let the temptation cycle begin for a prosperous and sinful Friday.

When the sun rises there's an automatic playback of the heavenly inauguration that took place on my private bed. I suddenly remembered the numerous scenes I played. At 12 midnight I became Cinderella, but in my reality I was less clothed and only one glass heel remained on my foot as he swung my legs and body back and forth.

I felt like the Little Mermaid maybe because I link the Little Mermaid with swimming, but in my special case something wasn't swimming around me-but it was swimming in me!

If you rang the alarm as I slept like Sleeping Beauty, I probably wouldn't hear you, neither did I move an inch after he took care of my body in the most x-rated way possible. I thought I would break with all that aggressiveness he bestowed upon me.

Hmm, Snow White wasn't relatable per say and I'm not saying that based on skin color. I say that because the only thing close to being Snow White was the fresh substance he gave up when he released.

My queen forever holds the palace down and Mufasaa comes in my moist confessional booth to swag thru my temple, touching and sanctifying my inner dimensions. I have no emotions and apologies for the way I come alive when I climb or sit on his throne. It doesn't have to be my birthday before I make him my bitch . . .

71

183rd Street

There was a legendary era where three African
(Toni, Tyrone and Toju) roommates lived on 183rd
street. That house birthed unimaginable sexual ac-
tivities. It was a place where constant sexual activi-
ties took place, and dick appointments were sched-
uled very often. All three roommates and friends
were all gay and appreciated the girth and length of
a big black dick. They had so many stories to share
with me starting from the encounters with men they
met from popular gay apps. It was a comfortable
place where if they were expecting a guest they
would show each other the person's photo so as not
to step on each others' toes. There was literally a
dedicated table in the corner of their apartment
where they had a stash of condoms and lubes ready
for easy grabs. This was a studio apartment with a

separated kitchen and bathroom at the end of the apartment. It was a special place that if a man was ever outside their door waiting for one of them to come out, it was usually to be escorted to his car to get some slippery, sloppy head with some deep throat action, it was a dick date and not a dinner date. It was a living space where it was normal for you to wake up and the first thing you saw was your roommate on their knees sucking dick in the kitchen. If you thought the roommate or the guy he was hooked up with would scramble in embarrass-ment, then you are wrong.

The roommate would ask "what are you looking at?! Close the door" and would immediately put the dick back in his mouth.

Tyrone was the one who had guys flocking after him. He "bagged" men from clubs, bars and other social gatherings. Tyrone told me there was a time he invited a guy over to fuck and when the guy arrived, he decided to actually take it slow and get to know him instead. This was a guy who was a manager at a TV station. During the conversation he was having with this guy, his roommate Toni had texted him asking him to hook him up with a guy, so instead Tyrone asked his guest if he knew anyone. His guest in return boldly asked for a threesome, Tyrone refused but allowed his guest to have fun with Toni. It wasn't a big deal to Tyrone as he went to shower and allowed his guest and Toni to have fun. Tyrone and Toni's guest had fun in the living room. Toni only gave him head as there wasn't enough time to get fucked before the judgmental Toju came back home. Tyrone has expressed how insanely thick the guest's dick was that he had no option but to quickly put his mouth on before the guest changed his mind.

Toju, on the other hand, tried to make sure he crafted an image that didn't really say he was having sex like the other roommates, but really, he was just secretive about it. He would question their daily schedules so as to invite his hookups when Tyrone and Toni were out. In fact, there was a moment Toju tried to invite someone over while Tyrone and Toni were sleeping. His action plan was to get fucked in the bathroom while his roommates were in deep sleep. He had sent the person the address and when the person arrived standing 6"5 tall, he was ready to go as he had been salivating over the person's 6 packs, dark skin and long dick that was sure to make a second hole in his bussy (boy pussy) after hitting his walls down.

As they walked in, the the guy he had invited suddenly said, "Wait, I was just here, earlier this morning".

After they talked and clarified the situation, it was known that Toju's guest had truly been there earlier that morning to fuck one of his roommates.

On nights where all the roommates had company coming, what they usually did was someone would use the living room, another person would use the bathroom and the third person would take a risk and get fucked in the hallway upstairs where the apartment was not occupied but locked. The one using the upstairs stairwell area would make sure to grab his essential gadgets so as not to interrupt his roommates. The hookups who arrived at first may be turned off at the fact of fucking in the stairwell, but Toni had a way of pulling down his pants to lure

77

the person or tempt the person. Once the person grabbed or touched his ass, it was like a magic spell and before they changed their mind he would lead the way to the stairwell. Imagine kneeling and scratching your knees against that hard rug- but not caring because that dick in you was life and all that you needed to keep you sane at the moment!

They had moments where Toni would be getting plowed in the living, while his roommates waited in the kitchen. Tyrone's hookup had came over with his roommate and this roommate gave Toni the business. According to Toni, the guy was Puerto Rican, about 5'6-5'8 but was carrying a dick that looked out of place due to his girth and length. Till this date, Toni swears that was the best sex he had since a French man fucked him. He says this Puerto Rican guy made him cream for the second time in his life and he moaned while his roommates made noise in the kitchen with only the living room door between them. He says that day he believed in the saying "Never judge a book by its cover".

They had rare occasions where they all attended a sex party. They had walked about 20 minutes to the location only to get there and find out that the host was lying (claiming people where on their way) and really he was trying to have all of them to himself. That experience didn't stop them as they attended another one that had been well advertised and had porn stars there amongst the people. Each roommate had always been about condoms till that night. High off poppers, each one had dick in their holes without the proper protection, but they had dedication to the pull out method. They all had a special moment they remembered when they ran to the hospital after the sex party at 3 am to go get PEP. That night never stopped their love for dick as they were hit with Hurricane Sandy the following week. The authorities had advised everyone to stay home but Tyrone had other plans. Tyrone that day was like the person in the meme we may have seen online that says "through the rain, through the storm, I must find my way to get this dick and nothing can stop me". He left his house in the storm to actually babysit his long time friend's dog while he left to attend to an emergency. Tyrone was paid well for taking care of his dog with every inch that guy had. He plunged Tyrone well in and out and sent Tyrone back on the bus home and not even in a cab. The love for dick will truly make people do some crazy stuff.

Matrimonial Lines

Marcel was a college student who got good grades, and had support from his family. He pretty much had everything going on for him and he was thankful for his life. He lived in the dorm with about four roommates. There were three rooms in total. Two roommates in one room, another two in the next room and the third room, right by the kitchen, had a single bed of its own. There was, however, one thing that was missing in his life and that was some good dick! He had gotten online and met this man whom he had chatted with for, and finally they decided to meet up. They usually met during the man's lunch break and Marcel would leave class to meet him in his dorm when no one was around. Marcel described this man as having a muscular body, bald head, mustache, beard, super thick dick, big arms.

This man was about 54 and Marcel was 19 years old. You see, every part of that man was useful for Marcel, starting with his bald head, it was what Marcel rubbed on when he was riding this man as he faced forward while also getting his nipples sucked by this man. The man's muscular body was something Marcel marveled over as he continuously rubbed on and mentally kept saying "Thank you God". The muscular body was something you gushed over and kissed time to time in between other activities.

Marcel said he loved the sight of his big chest and that's why he slowly rubbed the man down till he got on his knees before this man and placed his lips on the man's thick dick that continuously released precum. Marcel sucked this man like his life depended on it. Even though he choked and gagged, he made sure to look up at this man's face and looked for the facial expression that gave him feedback on how well he was sucking him. This man would lift up Marcel's head while he was sucking him, looking deep into Marcel's eyes and pulling out his dick to slap it on Marcel's face. After a few dick slaps on Marcel's face, the man would forcefully open Marcel's mouth and spit in it. Right after this, he slid his dick back in Marcel's mouth. His beard and mustache gave a tingly feeling when he ate Marcel's ass out. He used his big arms to lock Marcel in one position, while he dicked Marcel down for the gods showing no mercy whatsoever.

The man had the kind of thick dick that after he pounded for several minutes or hours and he pulled out, the ass or pussy would be stretched wide open, would take on the size of his dick and would burp upon him pulling out his dick. He certainly did train Marcel well on how to take his dick whenever they met.

Little did Marcel know that the man he had been inviting over was married and had been removing his ring every time he knocked on his door. This married man had been dicking him down constantly and religiously for six months straight, and they met 2 - 3 times a week. Marcel found out about his marriage when they were having sex and he looked over to see the man removing his wedding ring and putting it on the table. This happened right after he was fingering Marcel and maybe as he was admiring Marcel's wet hole, he decided to place the ring down to not feel guilty. They continued to fuck even though they had a conversation about it. Marcel was hooked on someone else's property at this point and the man got comfortable as he added weekends to their meet ups. There were days when he would leave his kids (teenagers) in his car while he went up to fuck Marcel so well, he would go to the married man's vacation house, walking by the man's son and going into the room with the man for hours. He said every time he came to the vacation house the son would be playing video games and would see him entering the room with his dad and would carry on with his video game. The wife was no where to be found.

Marcel graduated from school and had to leave that city and with that he had to leave the man. Before he left he had begged the man to fuck him on his rooftop of the dorm in the middle of night before he left for the airport. Things got so intense, that for the first time, the man went in raw and fucked Marcel as Marcel's leg was hanging by the edge of the rooftop. They both wanted a dare devil experience, so they fucked on the rooftop by the edge where he fucked Marcel passionately and was even shedding tears while doing so. The man sprayed his nut all over Marcel's face and as they went back to Marcel's apartment to clean up, the second round continued in the shower. He fucked Marcel again in the showers despite hearing the roommates opening the door in the hallway, but they had nothing to lose at Marcel was moving out by dawn and the roommates didn't know who the man was. It was the first time they knew Marcel was gay as he kept it on the low and was a pretty masculine guy. Till today, Marcel

says he searches online to find the man whenever he
came to town but could never find the man online
and the number he had for him didn't work any-
more.

Magun

Lolade was a well packaged lady from Nigeria. She had the full front, full hips and had ass for days. For some reason, men still would cheat on her as they never were satisfied. During her school days even she wasn't a saint. She remembered when she would be placed on the teacher's table and was given mathematics, science, economics, government, history lessons and more, straight into her tight pussy. Not only were the teachers being satisfied, but she also attended to some of her classmates, as well as seniors. Despite her promiscuous nature, she did yearn for love. Her boyfriend back then in high school was half Jamaican and half Ghanaian. She told him everything about her past so as to be totally open and transparent with him. For this he promised to protect her, cherish her and always be by her side.

The way he fucked her, she mentally couldn't keep the thoughts of his enormous black dick off her mind. Imagine being in the class setting constantly rubbing your legs, lifting your skirt and then using your school pen to finger yourself in the back of the class. At times, when he had a certain subject with her, he would be the one lifting her skirt at the back of the class, while the teacher was teaching and the students were paying attention and didn'teven notice them at the back. He would lift her skirt with one hand and with the same hand he would finger her for a few seconds. He then proceeded to take his finger out and place it in his mouth licking his fingers, getting it wet just to insert it back into her vagina.

It must have been very hard to keep quiet at the back of the class without moaning when being fingered like that. Her pussy was simply not enough for him to stay put, he decided his dick needed different kinds of other tight holes. He broke her heart and she has never been able to trust any man ever since.

Lolade had a long break away from dating or even having sex with any man. She had access to toys which were her satisfaction during that period. Wanting to date again, Lolade searched for what she could use against any man that cheated on her after she graduated college. She had asked her neighbor, who was very enlightened on things going on in the community. Her neighbor took her to where she could get a charm called "magun". This charm is used to punish anyone who rapes the buyer, is used to keep partners from being unfaithful and restricts a man or woman who is promiscuous. Typically to get this magun onto the person, a thread or broomstick is placed on the floor without the person's consent and once the person walks over the threat or, he or she would have the magus placed on her. So for example, a man can get the charm, place it on the woman, and once the wife walks over it, she would have the magun on her. If the wife went out to cheat on her husband, several things could happen from unexplained sweating, weight loss, strange illnesses that the doctors can't identify, they would have bumps and boils all over there body, have headaches, crow like a rooster, bark like a dog, have enlarged private part that are unbearable to the touch and sometimes could even die immediately. The most common one seen on TV shows is when the partner cheats on his or her partner, the cheater gets stuck to the person who he or she is cheating with. In other words, the person's dick will get stuck to the vagina of the person he is cheating with, and there is an unbearable pain while they are stuck. Only the partner's wife or husband can come cancel the spell to separate them from being stuck.

Lolade got this charm through her neighbor for a man she was dating. She strategically placed it on him of course without his consent at the entrance of her bedroom. They dated for years and everything was perfectly fine; she let her guard down and trusted him. They both had great jobs and moved into their dream home which they built from the ground up after purchasing land in Lagos. They got married and had 6 kids (2 set of triplets).

Just when everything seemed great, her husband disappointed her. He thought what he had at home was not enough or was no longer interesting. Just when he stepped out of his marriage, he got his dick stuck in someone else. His dick got stuck inside the ladies private parts. They both reached out to the neighbors after they screamed for help. Nobody could separate them and the pain was excruciating. He finally reached out to his wife Lolade and told her where he was at the moment. Upon hearing this, Lolade rushed over; she had forgotten the magun she put on him a longtime ago. When she reached there, she was even more shocked as she found out that the lady he was having sex with was her mother. Her husband was stuck to her mother, it was a sight no one would have hoped to see.

I still wonder if someone who has magun on them
could get away with foreplay.

3 is A Crowd

Lilly is a Filipino woman in her twenties. She is a lady with a shape to die for. Looks great in a swimsuit, she was a long hair don't care kind of lady. She just moved to Chicago to settle right after college. Little did she know her life would be a circus as she settled in.

Conversations with Lily

Lilly - Why is it so hard to let go of a man you know isn't good for you?

Me - Because we have been searching and when we find "sometimes trouble" we don't want to let go. We know if we let go we will be going back to our alone state. So we sorta have a "he will or might change" in the back of our head while we continue to deal

with the person. We have to realize our mistakes
and do much better with who we give our hearts to.

From this discussion, you would think Lilly would
have avoided trouble. She decided to dive into sev-
eral flavors of trouble- vanilla, chocolate and an ex-
otic kind of flavor. Lilly was dealing with three men
all together. The first one I referred to as vanilla
was named Mike. He was a Caucasian man that
looked like a Greek God. Light blue eyes, dirty
blonde hair, about 6"3 in height. He was a profes-
sional man and a lawyer. He always won cases ex-
cept the one with Lilly. He tried his best to keep her
to him and only him but she wasn't satisfied. He had
just gotten out of a relationship, in fact a marriage
and was at the point of looking for love again. He
had given her a ring to let her know he was serious
about her but she wasn't too sure if it would work.

He was a bit controlling and would try to tell her to change her clothes or try to know her whereabouts.

Lilly knew how to handle him when he talked too much or was misbehaving. It was as easy as grabbing his head and lowering it down on her vagina. Putting her pussy on his lips, this made him realize she was in control. Mike was the man that ate her out so well that she didn't need dick afterwards. Though he tried to dick her down, she would reject the offer after he ate her out and would leave him rock hard as she left his apartment. She never really took her clothes off for him, she would wear dresses or skirts purposely. It was as easy as lifting up the skirt or dress with no panties underneath and lowering his head into her sanctuary. He was a man that swiped his nose across her vagina giving each nerve a spark or an alert. This was always before he proceeded to glide his tongue all over her vagina with major concentration on the clitoris.

As he performed his duty on her, he also stimulated her mind, body and soul. She would close her eyes and get lost for a few minutes like an out of body experience, in fact, he would stop to see if she was ok and the response was always pushing his lips back onto her pussy.

Now the chocolate guy in her life was named Otis. Otis was medium built with defined abs, full beard and mustache. He was about 6"5 in height. Breathtaking smile and no matter what he wore, he always had a print pushing through his pants. He was a manager at a cable company and on the side he was a personal trainer. Lilly met Otis from an online app. Otis was a gentleman outside, but a bedroom bully behind closed doors. Otis's dick was the biggest dick she had ever had in her life. He had that ruin my life kind of dick, the kind of dick you travel to another state for, the kind of dick you called off work for and the kind that took away your common sense.

It was thick, long and it tasted delicious. It could barely fit in her mouth and it could barely fit in her tight vagina. It was one of those dicks that you willingly slapped on your face on your own before he did. You looked at in awe and went ahead and slapped it on your lips, forehead, nose and more. It was so gorgeous that you had to sniff from the bottom which is the pubic hair and balls. Otis was a freak and he gave Lilly her first tea bagging experience with her mouth wide open. He would insert his dick in her mouth watching her gagging, choking with tears rolling down. She was not allowed to use her hands at all, if she attempted, he would slap her hand out of the way.

Otis took his time to admire her precious pussy when she laid down. He would blow smoke on her pussy from the weed he was hitting or smoking. You see, when he fucked her it could barely fit but he somehow got it all the way in her. She thought she would die with the way she kept screaming and grabbing on to the pillow or the bed post. Otis lasted a long time with sweat dripping both their bodies. He was the kind to sleep with his dick in her all night, so when he woke up he would pick up where he left off.

Now Jose was mixed; he was Brazilian and Puerto Rican. He was on the slim, with tons of tattoos that covered his body. He wasn't packing like Otis, but neither did he have the body like Mike. However,

he knew how to work her inner system till it leaked.

He was a famous photographer and was quite busy

but always had time for Lilly when she needed to

book him for a photoshoot. You see, Jose was sim-

ply a gorgeous man. He had a great smile, great per-

sonality, had swag. This was such a turn on for Lilly

that she had to book him a couple of times to even-

tually get what she wanted from him. They would

both flirt with each other during photoshoots but

this particular photoshoot was the touchdown. Lilly

invited him over to her place to take pictures in her

robe to execute her sexy housewife photoshoot. Un-

derneath the robe she had nothing on and it was

strategic that she had nothing on underneath. Dur-

ing the photoshoot she would tease him about the

other models he took photos of that were complete-

ly nude. She would drop her robe, bend over and

act like those models. It wasn't long before Jose's dick got hard during all the playful acts.

Once Lilly noticed it was hard, she would tease him and playfully grab it. Jose eventually couldn't take it any more and started to grab her butt with one hand, and as he wanted to drop his camera, she put it back on him. She pulled down his pants and told him to continue to take photos as she gave him head. Jose was in shock but did as she instructed. He took pictures of his dick in her mouth, zoomed in on the spit dripping from her lips as she sucked. Even when she laid on the floor, he would get on his knees in the middle of her and zoom in on her clitoris and took shots. She pulled him in closer and he inserted his dick in her. After a few strokes, he was already making facial expressions that suggested he would bust any moment. She pointed at the camera signaling him to take more photos of her face. He took photos of her breasts, her mouth wide open and his

dick in her pussy. His HD camera got every detail

of the precum coming out of his dick. It also cap-

tured the cream on his dick which was from her

pussy.

Like any man would, Jose dropped the camera to

concentrate and fucked her like his life depended on

it. He whined his waist and stroked her deeply with

cream dripping down to the floor. He was roaring

and she was moaning, they both made music to-

gether. He pulled out of her pussy and busted all

over her face. He made sure every last drop was re-

leased on her face before he kissed her and took one

last photo of his cum on her face. Her face was cov-

ered in nothing but cum except for her lips; even

when she pulled her hair back it looked like she

used gel for her hair with his cum. That image was a

work of art and he smiled and that smile said "my work is done here".

These three men in her life left her confused because each one slowly wanted to keep her for himself. They sent good morning texts, as well as good night texts. They took her out and they fucked her good every time. It was perfect till she lost herself. They ruined her life with constant dicking that she couldn't refuse and so she had to leave the city, one thing she said she regretted was not organizing a threesome with all of them together.

She already imagined one dick in her mouth, in her pussy and in her ass all at the same time. She said it would have been the best gift ever.

Hookup Swap

There was a guy Sammy had been speaking to online. They had been speaking for over three months and finally they agreed to meet up as their schedule had finally allowed. They had planned to meet at 10 pm and it was about 7:45 pm. Sammy had checked and it was going to take him two hours to get there, but he figured if he kept speeding he would make it in 1 hour 30 minutes. So he threw on sweatpants and a t-shirt, then rushed out the door grabbing his car keys. He was speeding to get to his destination and he got very comfortable with this particular speed as no one stopped him. He had passed this particular road and didn't pay attention to the speed limit. Suddenly, a cop car came out

of nowhere and was following him and signaled
for him to stop. The street was dark and not a
person was in sight walking or driving, so au-
tomatically he got scared. He started to fear for
his life due to the police brutality going on in
the country at the moment.

He parked properly and the police car parked
right behind him. The police officer came out of
his car and walked towards Sammy's car. The
cop basically told him he was speeding, his
break light wasn't working and he ran a red
light. The officer asked for his license and
walked back to his car. He sat in his car for a
little while and then finally walked back with a
ticket in his hand. Just as he was explaining
things to Sammy, Sammy then interrupted.

Sammy said : I don't mean to disrespect you, but you're the most gorgeous person I have seen.

The Latin cop smiled, then asked Sammy: Where were you going?

Sammy - You want the truth?

Latin cop - Go ahead.

Sammy - I'm actually on my way to a hookup in Joliet.

Latin cop – Wow, that's pretty far for a hook up.

Sammy – Well it's all I could find at the moment.

Latin cop - What if I said what you are looking for is in front of you?

Sammy – Ummm, you for real?

Latin cop - Follow me.

The police officer headed over to his car to turned off his radio and told Sammy to get in the car and they drove into a dark place. The cop got down to open the gates and then returned to drive further in. He parked and then got out and told Sammy to follow him.

He noticed Sammy was hesitant and so he assured him that everything was fine. He told him not to be scared. After turning off the car lights, he climbed up and sat on the car hood. As the police officer sat on the hood, he lowered his pants and whipped out his dick. Before Sammy could say anything, the officer grabbed his head and lowered it onto his dick. Sammy gave him head for about 10 - 15 minutes. The police officer was now ready for some ass. He got down and lifted Sammy onto the hood. Sammy climbed up a little further after pulling his pants down and put his body on the windshield. It was then he noticed that they were in a grave-yard parked over where some bodies were buried. Sammy prayed for forgiveness while he spread his legs and arched his back waiting for the police office to throw on a condom and climb the car hood also. The cop fucked him right on the hood of the police car. The officer pounded him deeply while he moaned loud. Anyone with a dick can give it, but it takes tal-ent to take dick. Sammy certainly had talent and made sure he worked that police officer's mighty pole on that car hood.

The police officer nutted in the condom and pulled out of Sammy's tight ass. They quickly dressed and headed back towards where Sam my's car was parked. The officer joked that he hoped Sammy wouldn't stalk him and Sammy thought it was going to be the other way around, especially since he took his info from the driver's license. Sammy got to know that the Latin cop whose name was Nick had a wife and two kids. Nick ripped up the ticket he had given him. He even went to the car to cancel some other info he put in the system. He told Sammy to fix his brake light and pay attention to the speed limits as he drove off leaving Sammy behind. Sammy unfortunately could not move as he could not find his car keys. Luckily for him, the police officer noticed he wasn't moving and reversed back to see if he was ok. It was then they noticed Sammy's car keys on the hood of the police car.

After being satisfied by a hot cop, there was no need to go to the original hook up. The original hook up seemed to have called several times by the time he looked at his phone. He felt sorry for the guy so he at least gave him some phone sex. He slept well that night checking off a number on his fantasy list:number 18 was having sex with a police officer.

He Said

Mentally, I'm drawn to a dude that can stimulate my senses, impel me to have a cognitive orgasm and a man that knows how to laugh. I'm allergic to ignorance and weakness on all levels.

Physically I'm attracted to all, anyone that has the ability to draw me in maybe with his lips, eyes, muscles, height, nice hands and feet.

Sexually, I can take anything I'm given, but I enjoy the immense penetration of a dude that can go deep; I love to feel my wetness and my internal explosion. My dominance and massiveness are deceiving, but I'm attracted to a dude that is assertive, freaky and massive in bed.

I prefer a dude that's man enough to use his skills and tool to deeply penetrate me to the point of making me exert internal wetness and maybe even cream, but I still have a weakness for a nice sized, fuckable ass.

Forbidden Care Plan

Juanita moved to New York from North Carolina. She moved in with family members in New York. After weeks of applying at retail stores and offices, she decided to apply to be a Home Health Aide (HHA).

It took about 2-3 weeks training for the HHA program. After she had received her certification, she was given a job. Her first client was a woman and the lady was a lot of work. Juanita had to user a Hoyer lift to move her, she had to bathe her, cook for her, clean her when she pooped. It was a lot of work, she eventually found a way to get out of the situation, and luckily for her the client was quite troublesome. The client had a nasty reputation for throwing things and saying extremely rude things as well. Juanita called her office and told them she

117

couldn't handle the case anymore and they looked for something else for her. It took a week to find another case and this was an extremely new case. The client stayed in Lower Manhattan with his father. The mother had gone for a religious retreat and she had applied for care for her son. He could walk and do everything but just needed assistance to cook and needed company when the dad went to work. The first day Juanita reached the house, the dad was in a rush so she didn't get the full scope of what to do. Luckily, the care plan was left on the fridge and it said the client, whose name was, woke up pretty late and they let him sleep till he was ready to leave the bed.

Juanita kept her self busy and washed the dishes and mopped the floor in the mean time. She had gotten bored and sat at the dining table waiting for

Ralph to wake up. He finally woke up but came out of bed so quietly that she didn't even hear or notice him. He stood there without making a sound and stared at her, finally she looked up startled. She went to introduce herself to him, they got along just fine.

During Juanita's shift on a Saturday about two months later, Ralph had a fall in the shower. He was taken to the hospital and when they checked him he was totally fine just minor pain. However, it was suggested he relaxed more in bed due to his waist pain and back pain. Due to this circumstance, he needed help with getting into the shower and getting out. Sometimes he would need assistance to wash his back.

For the first time, Juanita noticed as she would assist him in washing his back or places he couldn't reach that his dick got hard, really hard! She would smile and avoid it, but it wasn't too long before things shifted from professional to personal. Eventually, Ralph summoned the courage one day when she was assisting him back into bed after his shower.

As he laid naked on the bed, he asked for assistance to rub lotion on his legs, she rubbed lotion on his feet and on his thighs. When she was rubbing lotion on his thighs he got a hard on, grabbing her hands and placing them on his dick.

Juanita was in shock but at the same time couldn't get her hands off his dick. This clearly signified she was interested. She did say she was afraid and could get in trouble but he assured her that no one would know. It wasn't necessarily what he said that convinced her, but it was the sight of his dick getting bigger and bigger. His dick was releasing precum

so much, signifying how bad he wanted her.

She told him it had to be a secret and it would hap-

pen only that one time. She looked at the time and

realized his dad would be back home in a few, so

she decided to skip the process of giving him head.

She climbed on top of him using the railings by

each side of the bed for support. Slowly, she sat on

his dick and he moaned out loud, she had to respond

with a "sssh" sound.

She slowly continued to sit on his dick till it was

balls' deep and gently started to pick her pace. She

was being mindful of his waist pain, but from the

way he grabbed her waist giving her feedback by

fucking her, that said he was healing fine.

Juanita, who told him not to moan in return, was the

one moaning the more he pounded her while grab-

bing her ass and smacking it. He pounded her for

about 15 mins and during this time they both didn't notice she had been creaming all over his thighs and sheets. They didn't pay attention to the time either, but luckily his father was talking to someone in the hallway and was laughing loud.

Juanita hopped off him really quick and he grabbed her hand begging her to jerk him off because he hadn't nutted yet. She yelled at him and told him, "don't you hear your dad at the door; stop it". She dressed quickly and acted like she was compiling his laundry while he acted like he was dressing himself after his shower.

The dad walked in and immediately noticed a weird smell, and when he asked, they both acted like they didn't know what he was saying. He leaned over to hug his son when he noticed his son was struggling to get his shorts up; he assisted him then noticed a whitish substance on his thighs.

Father : Ralph, what is this on your lap?

Ralph immediately said : Oh, it's lotion.

He rubbed the whitish substance which was really
the cream from Juanita's vagina. It didn't go away
smoothly like lotion, plus it had a different smell to
it. The father looked at Ralph and Juanita strangely.

Father : Son, that's not lotion.

Ralph : It is, it's that cheap lotion you keep buying
from the dollar store.

Father : You sure?

Ralph : What do you mean? I have been using this
cheap lotion and I told you I didn't like it, but you
keep buying it.

Father : I am your father and I came to this world
before you. I am telling you that's not lotion, but
Papi, I'll go prepare your dinner. It's almost time for
Juanita to leave.

Ralph : Yea, do that, I don't know why you're argu-
ing over this cheap lotion. You're acting like you

work for the cheap lotion company or you own the company.

The father looked at him with a smile, then he walked away. Juanita clocked out of the place so quickly it was before her exact quitting time. The father asked her to wait that he wanted to discuss something with, but she ran off once he went to the bathroom. She called off a few times after that day as she was extremely nervous to return to work. Eventually, she returned and the first day upon her return she didn't see Ralph. The father notified her and so she thought she wouldn't have work for the day so she was nervous.

Father : He is with his cousins, today.

Juanita: Oh my, I have tell the office about this.

Father : If I were you I would not tell them, that way you can still get paid.

Juanita : Ok, I guess I'll clean in the meantime to keep myself busy till it's time to clock out.

Father : Actually, before you clean there is something we have to discuss.

Juanita : Is Ralph moving?

Father : Oh no, it's not that.

Jaunita : Oh, ok then, what is it?

Father : We have to talk about what happened the other day with Ralph and the white substance on his thighs.

Juanita : Oh! What happened? I left early that day.

Father : I think we both know what happened.

Juanita : Oh, he didn't like the lotion, I'm sorry. I'll get him another one with his card.

Father : Juanita! Mama, we can both play this game or I can call the office and tell them what happened. You can get in trouble you know.

Juanita : I'm so confused, what did I do?

Father : Ok, let me put it like this, are you fucking my son?

Juanita: OMG! Excuse me?!

As she was denying and acting shocked, the father brought his phone. He ignored what she was saying and went through his phone. He lifted up his phone and played a video for her to see.

As she looked closer, she recognized herself in the video. The video was from a hidden camera in Ralph's room that caught her having sex with him. Immediately, Juanita dropped to the floor and started begging and crying. Ralph's father, however, kept smiling and he told her he would keep quiet based on one condition. The condition was surprising to Juanita as she figured he would ask that based on how he was smiling and had been acting around her since she started the job. Ralph's father wanted to have what his son enjoyed that day.

Juanita was far from rejecting the offer, and as she was trying to save her job, she also couldn't resist him. Both the father and son were attractive men. The father, asked for a little more than the son and compensated for it. He not only wanted to penetrate her, he also wanted to go through the backdoor. It was new to her and she had never tried it. It felt so painful to her especially the first time he got excited and shoved his large penis into her little hole with no ease. She did bleed a little bit that day and the next time he wanted to try it he went very slow. His dick could barely fit in her mouth, so when he was fucking her she would be feeling intense pain but pain is pleasure so she felt it was a challenge to take on. He also gave her poppers to use and assured her it would be less painful the next time he slid into her asshole. Poppers is a drug that helps to make anal sex so much easier by relaxing the anal muscles, making it less painful especially if your partner is big or you are just not used to anal sex.

The only thing the father did to make up for this pain was to give her $650 cash per week. He fucked her so many times that the money she thought she was making didn't even seem to be enough. Her pussy and ass hurt from the constant pounding from the father and the son. She eventually got tired because it no longer felt like she was coming to work, it felt like she was going to a whore house to get fucked. The son at least had compassion and asked before they had sex, but the father used the video to threaten her constantly. He also would fuck her so harshly as if punishing her for that incident; he also never nutted quickly so it felt like forever to her. Juanita I thought would have left the job after going through all these things but she shocked me when she told me that the father had a birthday party and part of his planned activities was to have four of his friends including him run a train on her. She said she was tired of the constant sex, the guilty feeling of betraying the company rules, as well as sleeping with a married man as the wife was on a religious retreat. However, she felt it was part of her fantasy to have men run a train on her so she took the offer.

That day came, and as she walked in, the father told her that his friends would be dropping $1000, so all together she would get $5000 dollars including the money from him. The location was elsewhere, but he organized a taxi to take her to the airbnb that he rented for the day. He also arranged somewhere for Ralph to be as well.

On reaching the location, she changed into the
clothes she was asked to wear. An hour later, she
received a call that they were coming upstairs.
Ralph's father had asked Juanita to be creative with
the way she attended to everyone.

Once she heard a knock on the door, she immediate-
ly got into character, starting with getting on her
knees. She opened the door while she was on her
knees with her lace & leather underwear and bra on.
As all five men including Ralph's dad walked in,
she instructed them to pull down their pants. She
started with Ralph's dad shoving his dick into her
mouth, she sucked and teased his balls. She spat on
it and stroked it while she sucked it again. The men
were making "oooh" and "ahh" sounds waiting for
their turns. She then grabbed two of the next guys
by their dicks and pulled them closer to her. She got
greedy by sucking for about 10 seconds then re-

moved her mouth and sucked the next one for the same amount of time. She went back and forth between those two dicks then pointed at the remaining two to come forward. This time she tried to put both dicks in her mouth to suck, she tried for as long as she could till her mouth got tired. After she sucked both of them, she stroked them as she looked straight into their eyes. Before she could give them the next instruction, one of the guys grabbed her waist ready to shove his dick in her until the others yelled at him to let the birthday man go first. Ralph's dad didn't care as long as he got his nut, so they all lifted her and threw her on the bed. Each person took a part of her body. One of them laid underneath her inserting his dick in her ass while Ralph's dad inserted his dick into her pussy. One of the remaining three guys put his dick in her mouth and the remaining two put each of her breasts in their mouth. Juanita's body was really busy and no part of her was left unattended to. All of them switched positions, and the ones that were pounding her pussy and ass nutted in her. The next two who switched to the pussy and ass used the previous guy's cum as lube to keeping fucking her. Juanita's body felt strange, not only was she creaming, her pussy was super wet. She started to squirt through her vagina as the men all rejoiced hi-fiving each other. After a few minutes, the men all stood up above her and started stroking over her face. She thought the guys that first nutted in her were done but it wasn't so as they joined to stroke over her face as well. The men looked so beautiful according to Juanita as she looked at each one of them using all their strength to stroke their dicks with their perfect-ly sculpted bodies. Their chests kept jumping, they had great things, their balls jiggled, they were on their tippy toes and their asses looked firm. Suddenly, it came rushing down on her, cum after cum, like a faucet. She got blinded as the first shooter got some cum into her eyes, so after that moment she just kept her eyes shut and all she could hear was moaning and loud "argh" manly sounds. Still she kept her eyes closed and all she could feel were heavy drops hitting her face, hitting her breasts. She even got some in her mouth as she had her mouth opened. She was covered in cum and no one would get her a towel to wipe her face.

When she called out for someone to get her a towel, she was interrupted by Ralph's dad who said "Juanita, I put the money on the bed and btw my wife and I no longer need you to take care of my son. I'll call the agency to let them know."

As she was in shock and was trying to get her thoughts and words together, she heard the men leaving and the door closing. She felt used, she felt embarrassed, but as she told me this story she was smiling. I guess this meant she loved the once in a lifetime choo-choo train express.

Desperate Measures

I've always heard of people who travel for sex.
People who call off work for the pipe. Guys and
girls who wait by the phone all day for the dick as
this particular person was quite special. His name
was Lanre. He was a cook and was popular in his
neighborhood. He cooked for high class individuals
all over Nigeria. What people didn't know was be-
hind the scene he was a full blown hungry power
bottom. Lanre wanted sex, if possible, and any-
where. Sometimes, he didn't even care how the per-
son looked as long as they were willing to fuck.
Mechanics, gatemen, bus conductors, politicians,
married men, school teachers and more knew him.
They had all satisfied him during moments when
he was desperate for sex. Even when he couldn't

find someone available he would pay a hustler or a struggling desperate university student to fuck him.

Over the years he became uncontrollable. Even when he expressed that he was molested by his uncle, I felt sad for him. Unfortunately, he confessed that he had been trying to reconnect with his uncle to get a confession, apology and to have sex with him now that he was older. I have never been so speechless and it's not the first time someone has expressed their sexual fantasy with sleeping with the person who molested them when they were younger.

Lanre was not able to get his hands on sex toys-for example a dildo- in Nigeria and so he used what was around him. It first started when he used the food items around him that were supposed to be used to cook. He used cucumbers to satisfy himself when he couldn't find someone to give him dick. In fact, he even used corn! He would take the husk off the corn and use the corn in him in and out till he nutted. I thought this was extreme, but it was nothing compared to what he did next. This really took the height of it all.

At times, there was a shortage of dick-in other, too many bottoms and not enough tops. The tops become picky even when you hit them up. Tops at times also don't like recycling the same bottom, they want a fresh hole. Once, he was in a place where there was scarcity of dick. Lanre texted his contacts, offered money, did everything possible to get dick. Part of the reason for scarcity was that word on the street was that he was a power bottom and people started to avoid him. He couldn't take it any, so in the privacy of his home that he shared with his, he grabbed a large beer bottle. He rubbed vaseline on the beer bottle and went ahead to insert it into his hungry and starving hole.

He pushed in it as far as he could, then he placed in on the floor and sat on it. Then he switched positions again and got on the bed to continue to insert it in as far as possible. As he was reaching his climax, his mum walked in he door. It was a sight she never wanted to see. She already wasn't ok with him being gay, but to see him with a beer bottle up his ass was another story. She yelled and screamed, regretting she gave birth to him. She walked out in disgust and locked herself in her room crying and asking God where she went wrong as a mother. Soon after, she heard Lanre yelling. She came out to see what was wrong along with the visitors in the compound. They found him on the floor bleeding. The bottle had broken up his butt and the glass pieces were cutting him. Out of embarrassment, the mother refused to follow him to the hospital. Lanre himself was embarrassed especially when he needed to explain why a beer bottle had broken in his butt-hole.

After he explained to the doctor, it wasn't long before all the nurses told each other what happened. From the nurses it got out to the streets. Soon, people knew what happened to him and he lost clients that he cooked for. Even though he was still healing after leaving the hospital, he had to move to South Africa to get away from the embarrassment.

Skin Tales

20/11/2003 was the first day Tobi had his male on male experience and it was also the first day he messed with a girl. He seemed to enjoy his male on male experience a bit more. He was at a house party when this all happened during a summer break from school. After holidays he started to notice that there were a huge number of guys who have had a male on male experience. Not all will admit it, and some even think about it but never try it. In Tobi's school, the dorms were separated, the girls on one side and the boys on the other. But during class sessions, both boys and girls were together as well as for lunch time.

Tobi was loved by all his teachers, classmates and more. He had good grades and never got into any trouble. He secretly had a few male crushes but never acted on them. His crush slowly transitioned into reality when the school accepted a particular male student into the school.

This student's name was Obinna, and he had transferred schools as he was running from embarrassment. He had repeated class so many times from his previous school that his parents decided to transfer him to shield him from the daily embarrassment. In addition to the embarrassment from teachers that pointed him out in the class, his classmates would use it to insult him leading to physical fights. He had a popular name and song they sang for him. They called him "Father Abraham" in reference to his age and being the oldest in the classes he had to stay behind in after repeating. They even sang a song for him which was actually a well know Christian song in Nigeria. So whenever it was sang during praise and worship, he felt very sad.

The song goes -

Father Abraham had many sons
Many sons had Father Abraham
I am one of them and so are you
So let's just praise the Lord
Right arm!

Father Abraham had many sons
Many sons had Father Abraham
I am one of them and so are you
So let's just praise the Lord
Right arm, left arm!

Father Abraham had many sons
Many sons had Father Abraham
I am one of them and so are you
So let's just praise the Lord
Right arm, left arm, right foot!

Father Abraham had many sons
Many sons had Father Abraham
I am one of them and so are you
So let's just praise the Lord
Right arm, left arm, right foot, left foot!

Father Abraham had many sons
Many sons had Father Abraham

I am one of them and so are you
So let's just praise the Lord
Right arm, left arm, right foot, left foot
Chin up!

Father Abraham had many sons
Many sons had Father Abraham
I am one of them and so are you
So let's just praise the Lord
Right arm, left arm, right foot, left foot
Chin up, turn around!

Father Abraham had many sons
Many sons had Father Abraham
I am one of them and so are you
So let's just praise the Lord
Right arm, left arm, right foot, left foot
Chin up, turn around, sit down

It was actually a nice song that got you to move and dance. I remember it from my high school days as well and in church also.

Tobi never really spoke to Obinna in the beginning, as they were not in the same class but they crossed paths during lunch time and in the dorm rooms. Obinna always teased him for being a rich kid and his general actions. He always came to Tobi's room also to visit his roommate whose name was Ike.

Obinna and Ike were very close friends so he was around in the room a lot visiting. This was how the hidden attraction between Obinna and Tobi started as they saw each other often. The day came when Obinna came over to a house party Tobi and Ike were having off campus during their summer break. The party was happening at Ike's house and some guests were already present playing games, drinking and more. Ike had to run a quick errand to the store so he left everything in Tobi's care. Obinna let himself into Ike's room located upstairs while the party was downstairs. Tobi told him Ike ran a quick errand thinking Obinna would leave, but instead of leaving, he decided to stay and wait. While he was waiting, he started to tease Tobi once again about being soft. Tobi responded by hitting him and Obinna hit him back. It became a physical battle as they wrestled. It started with him twisting Tobi's arms behind his back and pushing his head lower and in this position Tobi's butt poked out. While Tobi was in this position, Obinna stood right behind him too close with his pelvis resting on Tobi's butt. He made him beg to be released as Tobi's dick got harder and harder, poking through his football shorts. After a few minutes being in this position, he then released him. Immediately, Tobi once again hit him purposefully as he noticed his dick was hard in his shorts.

This time when Obinna grabbed him, he put him in a choke hold and once again leaned into his butt with his dick tapping his butt as it got hard through his shorts. They both fell down and rolled onto each other on the floor, kicking and slapping each other. Tobi grabbed Obinna's waist with both arms locked and his face on Obinna's pelvic area. He then pushed him against the wall and while they were in this position, Obinna was slapping his back. As Tobi was taking the pain, he was also busy sniffing Obinna's private area through his shorts as he still had him in a lock with his arms around his waist and face in the pelvic area. Obinna was able to gain power once again from that position to turn Tobi forward and put him back in a choke hold. He leaned extremely close and backed up still having Tobi in a chokehold and they slowly lowered each other to sit on the bed. As they lowered each other in the exact position they were in, it required Tobi to sit on his hard penis but because clothes were still on, it didn't fit or feel right and hurt as Tobi's fat ass bent Obinna's dick to the side. As he released him out of the choke hold, Obinna's dick poked out from his shorts with the mushroom head of his dick showing, giving a "peek a boo" tease.

Tobi immediately noticed the beautiful sight of his dick with precum oozing out. He couldn't resist himself but at the same time he didn't want to get beaten up for being too forward. So still in the same playful mood, he grabbed Obinna's balls and begged to be released. Immediately, Obinna did as he was begged and stared right into his eyes and Tobi knew he was going to get punched.
Obinna lifted his hand and Tobi closed his eyes ready for his punch or hard slap but he actually felt a touch on his ass. Obinna grabbed his butt then actually put his hands in Tobi's shorts to grab a hand full of his bare ass. With his other hand, he used it

to lower Tobi's head in the direction of his dick. Automatically, Tobi released his strong hold on his balls. Obinna whipped out his dick and placed it in Tobi's mouth. It was Tobi's first time having a dick in his mouth, it smelled kinda musty after the rough wrestling match they had and the precum tasted salty. They both were silent as they commenced their sexual ceremony.

In shame, Tobi couldn't look at his face but he kept sucking Obinna's cock just visualizing in his head the way the women sucked dick in the blue films he had seen. It wasn't long at all before Obinna in extreme excitement nutted in Tobi's mouth. Tobi pulled his head back and Obinna grabbed his head to stop him till he released every drop in his mouth. He thought the precum was salty, but the actual cum was another story.

During their session they both were, so now that Obinna's had busted in Tobi's mouth, Obinna had three words for him. First he said "relax" after he nutted in his mouth to calm Tobi down who seemed freaked out by the cum in his mouth. The second and third words were "swallow it" and Tobi did just that as he was instructed to do.

Immediately after, Tobi stormed out the door heading to the bathroom to gargle some mouthwash. On his way to the bathroom, Folake, a girl who liked him and who he also had a crush on, stopped him trying to get a kiss from him in the hallway. He actually avoided kissing her mainly because he still had a lingering taste of fresh cum in his mouth. He told her to hold on and rushed into the bathroom to gargle some mouthwash.

As he was finishing, Folake opened the door and let herself in. He tried to stop her as she seemed to want to get busy in the bathroom with the way she was grabbing his dick and she placed his hands on her breasts. Tobi never nutted when he was with Obinna, so he was still horny and thought "why not?".

He pulled up her skirt and lifted her onto the sink. Even as a virgin he acted like an experienced person and he was basically going off what he had seen from the porn movies he had seen. Just as he was about to slide into her while she was on the sink, she took a condom from her bra. He struggled to put it on and with her help he was able to put it on properly as she seemed to know more than he did. She grabbed his dick and put it in her and he just moved it in and out. He wasn't too confident in what he was doing, but she seemed to be enjoying it as she moaned. He covered her mouth so no one from the party would hear her.

Before she could cum, someone aggressively knocked on the door and he also heard Ike's voice also calling his name. They had to stop even though she was begging him to continue since she was close to cumming. Tobi returned to the party and Folake never spoke to him again as she resented him for leaving her hanging when she was close to her climax.

Tobi avoided Obinna when they resumed school, but unfortunately, he wasn't easy to shake off just like that. He met Tobi in the shower room one particular night after lights out when the majority of the guys were sleeping and forced himself on him. Right there in the showers, he gave Tobi his first experience as a bottom. He did warn him that it would hurt but he would go slow. He turned on the shower and let Tobi get wet, especially his back area. He then grabbed a bar of soap and rubbed it on his dick as lube, he also rubbed some of the soap on Tobi's hole as well. Just as Tobi breathed in and out, Obinna slid in him right there under the showers.

He went in slowly, making sure Tobi took all of him till he reached his guts, then he began the process. Tobi was in pain but loved feeling it inside of him, so Obinna went from mild to wild with the soap he had used as lube gushing out of Tobi's ass.

He kept pounding him in the showers in pitch dark during lights out but the sound of Tobi's ass clapping on his dick caught someone's attention. Someone heard the noise and was wondering what it was. The person kept following the sound till he reached the showers. Both Tobi and Obinna didn't even notice anyone around. They kept fucking and the person was watching, stroking his dick as well. The

person said "well done" and immediately they both
looked around as Obinna pulled out of Tobi's ass.
It was their classmate whose name was Franklin
who secretly had a thing for man on man action.
They both were silent at first and started to beg him
to not tell anyone. They offered money, offered do-
ing his assignments and other things they could
think of. He said no to everything and told them ex-
actly what he wanted. He told Tobi to bend over and
told Obinna to be a watch guard for them both. Tobi
was mortified as this wasn't the way he dreamed of
his first male penetration experience.

Franklin was actually cuter than Obinna, in fact,
Franklin had both school girls, and even female
teachers, lusting over him. The main thing bother-
ing Tobi about this situation was that his dick was
way bigger than Obinna's. It reached into his guts as
well, but poked his wall which was not the best

pleasurable pain. Franklin showed no mercy when he fucked him with the shower turned off. He fucked like it was pussy except this was a bussy (boy pussy). He fucked like he was releasing all of his school stress on poor Tobi's tight hole while Obinna had to hear him moaning. He fucked him so hard that his hole was unrecognizable and stretched beyond recognition.

Tobi thought he would have done a pull out method, but Franklin comfortably went ahead and nutted inside of him while roaring. When Franklin pulled out of his ass, all that was heard in the pitch black was the cum from his ass dripping and hitting the wet concrete shower floor. Franklin kissed Tobi on his neck, washed off and left. As Tobi was washing his ass, he felt a painful tingly sensation as he was using hot water. He said prior to his male encoun-ters he had researched to use hot water with a towel to gently massage the hole so it would close back up and regain its tightness along with a special substance called "alum". This was how he regained his tightness though he never used the alum.

For the remainder of his time in school he focused on his grades and even though he tried to stay out of trouble, trouble seemed to find him. He suddenly found more individuals in the school who craved male encounters. Surprisingly, it was the male students no one would have ever imagined. They were masculine, into sports, and had not only female attention, but had girlfriends. However, secretly they still craved a man's body to touch and more.

Uber Tales

I was on my way back home from an art show in Harlem. I called an Uber and I didn't know I would be in for a surprise. As soon as I got in I noticed the driver was extremely nice; we started talking about being from other countries and our experiences in New York.

He was from the Dominican Republic and he was a good looking guy, actually. When he started speaking about his experiences, I had to adjust myself and sit upright because he was spilling tea! He said his sexual encounters started when he picked up a lady from Long Island City to drop her off in Manhattan. When he dropped her off at her place in Manhattan and drove off, he looked in the back of his car and saw an envelope that she left. The envelope was sealed but had a sticky note on it that said, "Hey Mr.

Uber man, please use the items inside to come up-
stairs-I have a gift for you. Open the envelope".
He thought to himself that it was odd that she had
an envelope prewritten for him, but because she was
sexy, he wanted to see where this was going. He
even joked with himself that she was too pretty to
be that stupid.

Little did he know what was in store for him. When
he approached her building's lobby, the security
called up to confirm with her, and although he
wanted to drop the envelope in the front, the securi-
ty told him to go up.

In the elevator, he finally looked in the envelope
and it was her lace underwear along with her apart-
ment keys. He was stunned and confused but re-
membered how pretty she was. He reached her floor
which was the penthouse, he saw a note on the door

that said "open the door with the keys and let your-self in".

Although he was freaked out, he was still curious about what she was trying to show him or trying to do. He followed the traces of marks on the floor that told him to follow. The apartment was huge and had modern expensive furniture. The marks he was fol-lowing on the floor led him to the bedroom and there she was laying down. She was on the bed legs wide open with no panties and no bra, completely naked. She was rubbing her vagina, just waiting for him.

As he tried to take a step back to run, his key fell down. She then told him to come closer, to not be afraid, and he told her he didn't want to get in trou-ble that he was just going to drop the keys and leave. She just told him "nobody will know. Come here and fuck me please!"

He paused still thinking about it, but when he saw her fingering herself, he couldn't help himself. So he took off all his clothes in a rush; luckily he always has a condom in his wallet. He slid into her and she took a deep breath as he pushed further and further into her. He loved the sight of her pussy lips as they stretched open for his large tool.

He was still scared about the whole thing mainly because she was a Caucasian lady. He thought she may change her mind and scream that he was raping her. So before she changed her mind, he fucked her intensely. Each stroke was a deep and a hard one. He was stroking her fast, while grabbing a hand full of her breasts. He got excited forgetting all his worries, lifted her and placed her back on the sliding door to the balcony that showed the beautiful view to New jersey.

It was there he fucked her even more intensely than he initially was. She moaned loudly and he put his fingers in her mouth so she would suck on them. He then moved, still lifting her with her legs wrapped around his waist and her arms on his shoulders. He pounded her in the air so hard as if he was punishing her, so much so each time he pounded her it would make a splash. Her pussy was wet and she was creaming, so with every stroke it splashed again the walls, furniture and floor.

He then threw her onto the bed and moved her body into a doggy position. As he gave it to her from behind, he pulled on her hair aggressively. He thought he may have been hurting her but when she yelled " fuck me, daddy" he knew he had the free light to keep going. As he was about to cum, she got up and put her breasts together. He titty fucked her till he exploded on her tits, she then grabbed his dick and put it in her mouth to suck the rest of the remaining nutrients out of him. As his eyes rolled back, his toes curled and bones cracked, and as he stretched, she was showing her nasty side. She used her fingers to get some of his cum off her breast and put it in her mouth. She was creating bubbles with his cum smiling and looking at him straight into his eyes.

He had never experienced such in his life, so he took a deep breath and said "wow". She giggled, grabbed him closer to her and wanted him to fuck her again. He said he couldn't as he started dressing to leave. She told him he could come whenever he wanted, putting her business card in his pocket. He just smiled and ran out. He had to try to put his shoes on in the hallway as he was trying to escape her.

When the Uber driver reached my destination, he stopped and I was so into his story and escapades that I told him to tell me more quickly, but he actually parked the car and decided to dive into other tales.

He told me about a school teacher he gave a ride to that was flirting with him. He got her number, and after a couple of days, she finally invited him over. They had exchanged nude pics during their chats through text. So it was well understood what was about to happen, especially since she invited him over at 3 am in the morning. Like they say, "Nothing's open at 3 in the morning but legs".

When he walked in, she was in her robe, she didn't even ask him if he wanted water or anything, she just started kissing him and taking off his shirt. While they were kissing on the couch, she got up and told him to follow her into the bedroom. When she opened the door there was another lady naked on the bed. He immediately freaked out and panicked. She was able to calm him down eventually as he was already by the door. Apparently, the naked lady on the bed was her neighbor who needed some dick while her husband was out of town. In his mind he said to himself "Father, I made it" as he finally had the opportunity to have his first threesome, even though it came as a shock without prior notice. He then took off his clothes as both of the ladies got on their knees kissing each other and nibbling on each other's nipples. Each one of the ladies would take turns and suck him then kiss each other. One of the ladies laid down and the other lady sat on her face for her to eat her pussy and ass out. In that position, he laid on top of her and slid his dick in her pussy. While she was screaming, she was silenced by her friend's fat pussy on her lips.

He continued saying they both took turns to ride his dick to the point that he was exhausted. When he busted his nut on the neighbor pussy, her friend licked it off her pussy. Even when he went to shower to clean up, they came in there to join him and he had to fuck them again so as not to seem like a weakling to them. He said they wore him out to the point that he left the building limping to his car. He never reached out to her again after that.

One of his worst experiences was picking up a lady who was tipsy but still held a decent conversation. During the ride to her place, she flashed her boobs and talked about how much she loved sex. Even while he was on the highway, she reached forward to grab his dick while he was driving. He said he could have reported her, but because she was fine as fuck, he let it slide.

When he reached her destination, he turned off the Uber app and followed her in. Upon walking in he noticed it was a basement apartment. The apartment had lots of leather toys, cages, glory hole carvings through a door and more. They were cameras and immediately he noticed them, he told her that he forgot something in his car. She knew he was un-comfortable so immediately offered him a deal he couldn't refuse. She offered him 400 dollars to pee on her. For a moment, he just had a blank stare on his face because he never knew that was a thing. The money was tempting so he decided it wouldn't hurt after all; it wasn't his body. He told her he would do it but he would leave immediately.

So she told him to wait as she went into the bath-
room and got undressed to sit in the bath tub. After
about 5 minutes, she asked him to come in. He had
already unzipped his pants and before he got to the
bathtub she told him to pick up the money from the
sink. As he pulled the shower curtain to give her a
golden shower, he noticed she had no legs at all.
All along she had been wearing prosthetic legs
(which she placed in the corner of the bathtub), he
was weirded out, but since he has picked up the
money already, he just went ahead and peed all over
her face, hair, body and legs. She seemed to have
wanted to say something but he quickly zipped up
and yelled "bye" running out the door.

When he told me this all I could say was "wow" .
He did tell me he had repented and I said "hmm
mmm" with a little disbelief. He laughed and said

he has a girlfriend now so he left that lifestyle alone. I had to ask him if she was a customer he picked up during his Uber trips and he said she wasn't. I just hope no other customer he picks up will lead him into temptation especially if he is still doing late night driving.

Jackson Park and Parties

Tommy called himself a proud ho and he never was ashamed to admit to things. He was very open about his sexual encounters and more. He told me about an interesting place called Jackson Park in Chicago. It was a legendary place and probably still is.

He shared with me how he came across Jackson Park. He said he actually found out about it from a video he saw online where someone was getting pounded in the park. He scrolled down to see the comments and someone had mentioned the exact location which was "Jackson Park".

Tommy was curious to see if he would catch some-one getting fucked like the video and so he went to the location after doing his research. When he got there, he was let down. He saw police officers were doing an investigation. Apparently, there was an altercation in the park that led to someone being stabbed so they weren't allowing people to go into the park.

The next time he went to Jackson Park was during the black gay pride celebration. The black gay parade is separate from the main gay parade and its done during the day with mainly African American individuals in attendance.

A few people had left the parade and headed towards the Jackson Park area once it became evening. Tommy followed people that were heading towards the park. They approached the parking lot that he saw the last time he came there.

This time, people were standing around drinking, eating, dancing and more. Some people were in their cars getting head as Tommy walked by. The further Tommy followed them into the park, the trees got denser and it became scarier. Behind a tree

he spotted two black men; one was on his knees

sucking dick like his life depended on it. Further

down behind a big rock was a Spanish guy with a

black guy. The Spanish guy was getting pounded

for the gods, even as people stopped to watch they

both had no care in the world as they kept going.

Walking further by a little lake he saw an older

white guy getting fucked by a super slim boy that

looked extremely young. Tommy said the boy

looked young but the dick on him said I'm grown.

They couldn't even see the dick for too long because

the older man kept gulping it desperately. A little

further was a camera crew shooting a porn flick. We

tried to get a first view to this coming soon flick,

however a man that seemed like the director chased

us away because the immature queens behind us

kept laughing and giggling ruining the mood for the
porn actors.

Jackson Park was a place for anyone to cruise be-
fore the police officers or park security came. Walk-
ing past random condoms on the ground was a regu-
lar thing. The sight of cum or cream from one's ass
and vagina or even saliva from a blow job hitting
the fallen leaves or flowers was a daily thing at
Jackson Park. The smell of fresh cum mixed with
the cool breeze was everything to those that sought
pleasure at Jackson Park. However, since they
couldn't get or find some action at the park, they
decided to head to a sex party and Tommy tagged
along.

Tommy mentioned that when he got to the sex party
it was in the basement of a big old white house on
the south side of Chicago. They knew about this sex

party from someone who has received an invitation text. Upon reaching the party, he said it was 15 dollars to get in from someone who collected payment immediately as you walked in. There was a room right beside the basement entrance that everyone used to take their clothes off. It was required you were completely naked.

After taking off their clothes, Tommy followed them into the open area that was super dark with a pool table in the middle. There were men completely naked head to toe walking around feeling each other out to see if they were a match to fuck. It was so dark that it was possible to not even see the person bending you over and piping you down. The way to have seen people's faces in the room was when cars from outside drove by and their lights flashed across the room, that was the moment to quickly get a glimpse of who was in the room.

Some people were sitting on the pool table getting their dicks sucked, some laid on the pool table and were riding their tops. There were condoms available at each corner of the room in buckets, however it seemed like most of them just went in raw. The bottoms in there were pretty desperate for dick. About five bottoms would follow a top around the room in hopes he would grab one of them to fuck. Sometimes, they would even line up as he was fucking one bottom so that when he was done they were lined up waiting and he would fuck them one after the other.

Some of the bottoms would be getting fucked on the motorcycles the house owner parked in the basement. Tommy even saw someone getting fucked in the car trunk that was open.

The house owner had a couch in the basement as well with 3 bottoms kneeling on the couch bent

over in a doggie position as he ate them and pound-
ed them one after the other. He was not sharing
those bottoms with any other tops in there. It
seemed like he did advanced recruiting for those
bottoms to be there for his satisfaction only.
Tommy explored his wild side that night as he wor-
shipped each and every dick that poked out through
the glory hole that night. He deep throated every
inch letting the veins on their dicks rub again his
tonsils. He only stopped when he started to feel his
jaw line hurt, although he said usually he could go
on. But that night, so many people were packing
thick dicks.

Right after this, he put his versatile potential to
work- which meant him topping someone (giving
the dick) and also him bottoming (receiving the
dick) for another person. He nutted both times leav-

ing a mess on the owner's floor and left the sex party smiling from ear to ear.

He says he still goes to Jackson Park usually in the evening and for some reason married men were more present over there. The word on the street according to Tommy was that gay men suck dick better so the married men come to get their dicks sucked at the parks. He says he sucked their dicks first and asked questions later and that's when he usually found out they were married.

Barber Tales

Rod was a college student who found himself in Chicago. He worked two retail jobs while going to school. He had a roommate who also was in college, and his name was Mensa.

They were more like brothers as they had gotten so close over the past couple years. They knew practically everything about each other. Mensa was the one person Rod would take with him to an HIV test and to other private situations. He was like a person he would show his butthole without feeling ashamed if he had a bump down there.

During their friendship, Mensa had met someone on the south side who gave him haircut. He always had amazing haircuts and would always head to the south side to get his hair cut. Rod did notice whenever his roommate would get his haircut he would come back glowing and smiling extra hard. So he asked what was the deal with his glow when he returned from his appointment. Mensa told him that truly he gets a haircut, but he also gets a special treatment afterwards from the barber whose name is Eddie.

It all on who was at home at the moment and the package the client selected. The blue package was when the barber would professionally concentrate on giving the client a hair cut and then afterwards give good dick. The black package would be when the barber would cut the client's hair as he was completely naked, and the client was allowed to touch and even suck him while he cut hair in addition to getting fucked afterwards. This all seemed unsanitary, but the bottoms all seemed to be hungry

and not thinking about that. The gold package was
when the barber would include his friend who mas-
saged your feet and more while you got a hair cut.
They both were naked, the friend of the barber gave
the client some head while getting a haircut, then
afterwards they both fucked the client. The friend of
the barber was versatile, he was ok giving the dick
and receiving the dick depending on what the client
preferred.

The regular haircuts were like 15/20 dollars, but
with the extra, packages were like 80 dollars or
more.

Eddie got away with this usually when his cousins
were around and they would be the watchdogs to
alert him when one of his mothers or kids were on
the way. The barber had 4 baby mothers and 12
kids.

Rod eventually found his way over to the barber to get his services as Mensa didn't care. Rod signed up for the blue package, however the barber ended up eating him out more than he did anyone else. He texted Rod a little more frequently than he was supposed to. There were times he invited Rod over just to pound his cakes in his bedroom, which no client had ever seen because usually he fucked them in the living room where he cut their hair. He was falling in love with Rod and Rod loved the attention, except he wasn't ok with him fucking other people.

The more he went over to the barber's house, the more he planned with Eddie how to turn his basement into a barber shop. He helped him recruit about five barbers online. They would use the living room to cut hair and use one of the bedrooms for privacy and fuck the clients afterwards. They fucked the most masculine men ever, men in suits and ties, hooded guys, cops and politicians.

It was a money making business and eventually Eddie stopped fucking clients, including Mensa. He only did the professional hair cutting for people, which made Mensa feel excluded and left out. It felt like he cut off Mensa's dick source, causing tension in he and his roommate's house. Rod had to choose between Eddie and his friend Mensa. He seriously thought of the nights that Eddie would fuck him like he was the last man on earth, but because of the respect he had for Mensa, he let it go.

It was a good thing Rod stopped going there or speaking to Eddie. Things got messy at that location as someone got shot. The word on the street was one of the barbers hired was initially ok with the idea of fucking a guy for the money, but as it started, he felt grossed out and shot the client who was gulping his dick at the moment. Then he came out of the room shooting more people who were in the house. Like they say, not all money is good money and this was a lesson learned for Eddie who was lucky to be alive.

Jerking Off Diary

Have you ever jerked off to someone's pictures? I
mean your legs are shaking at the end kind of jerk
off. You find the sexiest photograph of them and
enlarge it on your laptop and sit or kneel right in
front of their picture. For a few minutes, you touch
yourself and look right into the eyes of the person's
photo on your screen. Then you listen to the moans
of the pornstars in the video you're playing in the
background. For some reason, playing three to four
videos at the same time makes it sound even better
as you listen to every sound. You put on your head-
phones and listen to ass clapping on thighs and a
dick ramming itself into an ass or pussy. You in-
crease the volume to the loudest it will go as you
listen to someone choking on a dick or listen to
someone spitting and jerking off.

For a few minutes, you stay put in the position con-
centrating on this photo that has been enlarged on
your screen. The friction and intensity increases and
you nut all over your laptop screen and keyboard.
Of course your upset by this, but you're also glad
you did it. I mean, it's your little secret that you just
nutted to your favorite crush-someone you would
let have you anywhere, anytime, any place and any-
how.
As you get up to clean, you have inner thoughts of
the possibilities of him or her fucking you real good
in person. You say aloud your inner wishes hoping
it they come true some day.

A Lustful Journey To Wet Island

With your super power, I want you to grab my ass.
Smack it, squeeze it, admire it and eat it.
With your tongue and my pussy, create a moist
prophecy before you insert your face in between my
thunder thighs. Lick your lips as you dive your face
in and be careful not to waist a drop. The pink fla-
vor is as sweet as skittles-as juicy as a starburst
candy. Feel the texture of my soft skin and do jus-
tice to my body. Your mine and I'm yours!

Let's get carried away and fulfill our sexual destiny
and when we are done we can then look up into the
heavens and scream "ahhh" passionately.
Before I go, sign your name with your magic stick
on my forehead. I was here, I saw and I definitely

conquered. I will be forever grateful for the great dick you have given me.

Welcome To Hornywood

I must say nothing is better than you gagging on my big dick, then assessing the weight of my big balls with your palms and fingers! Feel the texture to make sure it's what you've requested. I'm only 9 inches long, but inside of you it will feel like 12 inches! There is no amount of energy drinks that could help you get through this intense session. You will need a wheelchair from the damage done after.

Lick on my body like it was a do or die affair, grab my butt cheeks like a dollar bill was printed on my skin. Before I go into the main attraction I have to access the pleasure units.
Are the nipples on point like Hershey's kisses? Are the under lips wet like a watermelon?

I respect your tongue enough to allow it to bathe me with your natural mountain spring waters your mouth produces around my big dick. Then, maybe I can reach over and stimulate your pussy and fill it like an inauguration hall before I become your president. I see rehearsals aren't necessary for a professional, so let's shoot this award winning movie.

The red alert light is officially on, so it's my turn to make you cry your eyes out. Let me be your addiction, your favorite superstar. I want to earn my gold star on your Hollywood Boulevard. Then I will shoot my stars and blind you with my nutrients across your pretty face.

Community Dick

Oneal was a charming attractive man with dreds. He had a caramel tone and he was muscular. He had a breathtaking smile that stole your heart away and when he winked at you, your bra and panties would fall off before you knew it.

Oneal worked as a security guard and barely stayed at his duty post; he was seeking to enlarge his coast and upgrade himself. He was well aware that he was handsome and both men and women wanted him. He also gave them what they called community dick.

He had a full schedule of pussy appointments, he was booked and busy. If he fucked you once then you were part of his collection. His dick was so good that women lost their marbles and offered him whatever he wanted after laying that tremendous dick down. He fucked the boss at the job he was at, he fucked the dish washer and fucked a lady who was seeking asylum using her required job to help. They bought him a car, paid his rent, cooked for him, paid for his flights to other cities and more. He was loyal to no one and even almost got ran over with a car by his ex girlfriend whose heart he broke. He treated her badly, and even when both of her parents died, he wasn't there to console her. But he even made himself available to her sister and comforted her with his dick.

Oneal had met a mother and daughter at a local store during one of his shopping sprees where he spent the money he had gained from the numerous pussies he was servicing. The mother's pussy was experienced with knowledge, skills and more, while the daughter's pussy was a brand new sealed package that he was lucky to open up first. He fucked them both constantly and between them both he made lots of money. For the dick he gave the mother, he made her pay his rent, buy and cook for him. She was in love and he really only had feelings for her money and her experienced pussy.

As for her daughter, Oneal flaunted her as his girlfriend at events and more. She was also head over heels for him and Oneal had love for her expensive car, money, network and her friends. He was able to fuck her friends and benefit from them as well. A lot of people said that unless Oneal's dick was involved, he usually didn't care. Yes, Oneal was always thinking with his dick, but people didn't realize he was surprisingly thinking with his pockets as well; he had no boundaries.

Unfortunately for the daughter, she never knew why her parents got a divorce. It was known that her mother caught her dad getting fucked by another man. The mother immediately got a divorce and when the father came around they acted normal.

Oneal had come across the father one day in their mansion. They looked at each other in lust and eventually they found a way to connect with each other. The father was added to the list of people Oneal was dicking down. The money was his motivation for laying the pipe down when it came to the father he often said. The mother and daughter were ok sharing the same penis, but they didn't know the father was also bending over in a doggy position while getting his guts rearranged by Oneal's large dick.

Oneal made a lot of money from the whole family and he used it to elevate himself. He eventually gathered all the money he made from the whole family and other ladies and moved to another city to start a whole new life. He changed his number, moved out of his place and was never seen again. A lot of the women would have done anything for him to have been their life partner, but he settled down in the new city with a woman who didn't know any of his past. They do say everything hidden in the dark comes to light and Oneal was hoping and praying his wife never ever found out about his past.

Rock Bottom Sex

It's very rare that we watch countless porn videos and we get to meet our favorite porn star. We have saved tons of links of videos they have been featured on. We keep up on all there social media pages and have screen shots of all their nudes. We at times have spent plenty of dollars to even get their nudes. Some of us swear to ourselves, and maybe our friends, that when we have the opportunity, we will drop on our knees and get to sucking if given the opportunity or if the porn star even winks at us-the panties are coming off, its over.

Unfortunately, when Thomas had met his favorite porn star it wasn't the best experience, but he says he is still grateful for the opportunity to fall on his knees and taste the premium dick that plenty of men and women lust after online.

Thomas's favorite porn's stars name was Tyson "Bedroom Bully". He had been messaging him for about two years consistently on the gay apps. Tyson really didn't care to chat or look for love, he was mostly on the app for money whenever he was out of work from shooting more porn videos.

You see, it wasn't uncommon that some porn stars were escorts on the side. Name your price and they would be at your doorstep in minutes. The regular charge on Tyson's page was $300 per hour (regardless of if it was just oral or massages) and to sleep over was about $1000 plus. A lot of the porn stars offered massages which was more of a body rub down and lots of dicking by the end of the session which was the happy ending. Happy ending to most people was getting jerked off, but paying clients

with the bag got dick in them as their happy ending.

Thomas was lucky that night, because when he

messaged Tyson, it was a no cost situation. Tyson

responded to Thomas that he just needed to leave

the house and that he was bored. He did ask

Thomas if he had T (which means tina which is a

drug that is either sniffed, injected or taken as a pill.

It's known to get you extremely high, extremely

horny, energetic and most of the times comes with

hallucinations etc). Thomas lied and said he has a

man that supplies him tina (even though he had

never tried it in his life). He told Tyson he should

come over while he reached out to his supplier.

His mission was really to get "the bedroom bully"

in his presence. Bedroom bully noticed Thomas

stayed far away as they chatted some more, so im-

mediately Thomas offered to get him Uber to come

and to return before "bedroom bully" changed his mind. Thomas was extremely horny and felt it was a once in a life time opportunity to finally get a chance in getting that dick, so he was willing to do anything possible.

Thomas had mapped it and it cost about 35 dollars to get Tyson over. In about 27 minutes, Tyson arrived.

Thomas felt nervous that this might be catfish because he was in disbelief that it was really Tyson "the bedroom bully". He went downstairs, and to his surprise, it wasn't catfish.

Tyson unfortunately showed up high and was barely walking right or keeping his eyes open. He walked Tyson over to the elevator quickly before anyone noticed them.

In the elevator, Tyson suddenly whipped out his dick. In shock, Thomas was embarrassed, praying no one else got on the elevator. He even told him, "hey put your dick back in your pants; your gonna get me in trouble". There were no cameras in the elevator but he was scared that anyone could get on and see them.

Once the elevator reached his floor, Tyson immediately stepped out of the elevator with his dick still dangling out of his pants and said, "mehn, imma fuck you real hard, bro, for real". Thomas, in return, responded saying, "shhh stop it".

Immediately, they got inside the apartment and closed the door. Tyson then took off his clothes and asked for a drink. Thomas was afraid to give him a shot because he noticed he wasn't himself and seemed. But despite his misgivings, he still gave him vodka, and next thing he knew, Tyson forcefully bent him over and stuck his tongue in between

his ass cheeks. A part of Thomas wanted to stop be-

cause the man was clearly not himself and it seemed

like he was taking advantage of him, but the other

side of him was reminding him of how long he had

waited for this moment. He went with the part of

him that reminded him of how long he had been

waiting to meet Tyson "The bedroom bully".

Tyson forcefully arched Thomas's back as he dived

his face in along with his tongue. He was tasting the

soft part of his hole, sucking on the inner soft skin.

Then he proceeding to tongue fuck him aggressive-

ly with his saliva dripping down to the couch,

which he was bent over on top of.

With absolutely no warning, "the bedroom bully"

attempted to shove his enormous big dick in

Thomas's tight hole. Immediately, Thomas pushed

him back and "the bedroom bully" hits his hands away and pushes his dick in further. Thomas jumps a bit as bedroom bully's dick stretches his ass hole causing intense pain. He was luckily able to reach out for his poppers (which is an aide that helps the anus muscles to relax to receive penetration. It is usually sniffed and sold at the sex stores). After sniffing his poppers he felt like his body was no longer available or that he couldn't feel his body. He had a temporary high so even when "bedroom bully" inserted the full length of his dick in, it didn't hurt that much at all.

Bedroom bully pounded Thomas's ass like he was servicing a client that was generous with their funds. He fucked him with no mercy like he usually fucked his female porn star coworkers. It was going so well till Thomas felt he could take no more and felt a slight pain. Bedroom bully at that point was officially hitting where it wasn't supposed to and they had to stop. Upon pulling his dick out of his ass, it was a combination of ass cream and a bit of blood. Thomas wasn't surprised at the blood, after all he was being selfish knowing fully well that he couldn't take it but he was determined to get a pain in his walls that would make him remember bedroom bully for about three weeks or more.

Bedroom bully wanted to continue fucking regardless of the blood, but Thomas was smart enough to keep his hole intact and not ripped even further. It took about an additional hour after to get bedroom bully out of his house as he was extremely high, sleepy and hallucinating. Thomas till today says the dick and the pain was worth it. He even has a video and picture of bedroom bully going in and out of him. He has no plans to upload , but he watches it every now and then to jerk off. He never reached out to bedroom bully again because he was not so turned on by the drug use. Thomas says what he regrets the most about the situation is that he never got to actually taste bedroom bully's dick and take a selfie pic with it in his mouth. He said he did send him a message once, but bedroom bully left him on read. He says he still stalks him to see his where-abouts, but with bedroom bully's fan base, its going to be kind of hard to invite him over again or get his attention especially seeing that he jacked up his price from 300 to 750 per hour.

Jerking Off Chronicles

We don't take enough time to appreciate how much jerking off satisfies our current raging urge. Jerking off is the new way out of sex that's not actually sex especially with a partner who hasn't learned how to please us well yet. Jerking off is a private interaction with our own bodies and mind. We finish off on our own, no need for talking. Jerking off is a higher class in session with just our hands and our private parts.

There is beauty in searching through our favorite porn stars' names thinking of their tattoos, large dicks with veins, scruffy beards, arms, pink pussy, large breasts and more. Clicking on the bookmarked links of their videos is our secret passage into our own nasty world. The excitement is setting up our laptop and assembling all our toys right beside us so we don't have to make numerous trips around the house with our precious precum dripping onto the marble or wood floors. With the lights off and our headphones on the loudest volume, we start to play our videos that are lined up for the night. The extra topping is the saved picture up on our screens of someone we want to fuck so bad or someone we want to fuck us desperately. This is a private session so no one sees as you increase the size of the photo of this person you long for on the laptop. Closing your eyes for a few minutes, stroking your dick or fingering your pussy or inserting a dildo up your ass- the decision is yours.

The great tip to this personal session is stroking, fingering yourself and looking right into the eyes of the person's photo you have on the screen with the

porn videos playing in the background. You close
your eyes to take a moment to appreciate the female
porn star who is moaning and scream as her ass
claps on the guys dick. The moaning and dirty talk
from the videos is what makes a man rock hard and
a woman wet!

From mild to wild, we increase the speed and inten-
sify the pressure as you stroke your dick and finger
your pussy or ass. You lock your vision on the video
playing showing the zoomed in clip of the porn
star's dick intensely slamming into a vagina. The
cream splashing out of her pussy, the tears rolling
down her eyes, the veins on the man's dick, his pecs
showing, all of these aid to get the cum in your dick
and pussy find it ways out and explode all over in
the air. Some of the cum covers the lens of the lap-
top camera or phone that you're using, but this is a

sign of a job well done to please your body and give it what it deserves. Just make sure no one comes in with a UV light to inspect your private sessions, your filthy behavior, even though it's your private residence.

Sex Toursim

This is tea that I came across as I once sat in the living room of a lady who proudly talked about her sex tourism trips in Africa. She was from Europe but took many flights to Africa. She mainly deposited her funds into men's bank accounts who were less fortunate in these countries. She and her group of friends (some married) would take yearly trips to a particular country in Africa to get their engine serviced. They paid lots of money to these men. These men were their tour guides, construction workers (at the houses these women were building after purchasing lands), hotel check-in attendants or simply college boys who needed money to pay their school fees.

These women took care of these men and their families. The men had one major job which was to dick them down behind closed doors. They made advanced plans to meet different guys on a daily basis who promise to take care of them in the bedroom upon their arrival. You see, I got to learn that this sex tourism didn't just work for women seeking men, it worked for men seeking men as well. This is where the word bagsexual comes to light (gay for pay, men that are gay and will do anything for simply the money). I heard it's usually the women who feel they are not seen as attractive in their country that would travel to Africa to get serviced after paying top dollars or euros. They say money talks and those men's dicks are listening and tuning in to the radio station with the big bucks. These men were young, hung and looking for fun while getting paid for it.

Bagsexual

Sometimes I don't know what it is, but the tea al
ways gets delivered to my doorstep. So I thought I
would share this tea with sugar and not sea salt.
Bagsexual means a man who often claims to be
straight but is willing do anything or certain things
with other males for money, career upgrades or a
better social status. Bagsexual also means gay for
pay. Rub his head, stroke his ego, be desperate and
offer money, they say for a man who is bagsexual,
 they will fall right into the trap. Society today
says everyone has a price.

The Social media male models, fitness trainers,
your local weed man and upcoming music artists
are a few examples of guys who can be bagsexual

and sometimes have a price, especially when you slide in DMs or text them. Believe it or not, they sometimes have a wealthy man who is sponsoring their trips, education, careers, and even harder to believe, taking care of their wives and kids.

The OnlyFans website we think we know is not just an online content sharing platform for people who have fans. The content creators have made pages on OnlyFans that have become a gateway passage for other things. They get requests for custom videos where they show their butt to male fans, or even requests to show their feet. They even sell worn and cum stained underwear to customers and they use toys (dildos etc) in the videos for their paying male customers. They even charge for FaceTime shows where they do whatever the male paying customers ask them to do. Lastly, depending on how much you are willing to spend, you could meet them in person for a full course meal.

We often know of these guys that intentionally join gay websites just for the cash. They know guys will rush them with the dollars, so they go straight to the well and they do make loads of cash. Going in with no emotional attachments, they offer massages and more, depending on how much you are willing to spend.

People can now easily go on a website that offer men you can rent as a stripper for a bachelorette party, some of the men on there can be rented as a masseur and some men are there to be rented to come dick you down, plain and simple. They come in many flavors, shapes and sizes. They upload photos of their dick, and even have videos of them fucking clients for you to see what they are capable

215

of. These are the men that are flown in from other cities to satisfy someone's need. Some of these straight porn stars have a price and will go gay for an enormous check on the low. I am also being told that most fitnesss trainers or personal trainers offer escort services after the training session. They help you get in shape and proceed to work your hole and give it a work out with their big dick. Many men tell their wives that they are out driving Uber for extra money but really are driving into someone's tight hole. They click reject when their partners call as they are getting their dick sucked by a client who may have Ubered them over for a private session. Everyone has a price they say and this is very true these days.

Your tax returns are their pleasures, your stimulus checks are their needs and your approved grant money is their life source. Everyone has got to make a living.

Yoruba Demon

I knew he was married when he slide into my DMs .
However, it was my choice that he showed up to my
door step. A magnificent work of art from the moth-
erland, Nigeria to be specific. He was so fine, his
body was perfectly sculpted and he smelled so good
I couldn't help myself as I opened the door.

He started to feel guilty about coming over and I
started to get frustrated at him teasing me. So I got
up and showed him my healthy cakes and he
couldn't resist. I then grabbed his dick saying "I'm
sorry" and looking straight into his eyes with my
puppy dog sad face.

Then I proceeded to get on my knees and unzip his
pants and place his dick in my mouth. He was an

undiscovered fine ass man with a well crafted gold-
en dick. I had to take charge before he changed his
mind.

I started sucking him while I was on my knees, star-
ing up at him as he stood above me. It's so easy to
seduce a man, they say it's because they are weak
and love getting their dick wet. I'm just surprised
that nobody talks about the moment when they
change their mind mid sex.

This Yoruba demon was already deep in me, with
my pussy dripping juice to the floor. He then
stopped after few strokes to say "I'm sorry I can't
do this" and started dressing to leave. I begged him
to not leave and when he stepped out I even mes-
saged him to come back. The fool could have at
least let me cum before he left.

I later found out the reason why he left during our fuck session was because he had another woman scheduled that same day and time that he had been trying to get with for a long time. So, he left my pussy hanging to go attend to another desirable wet pussy. Unfortunately, his wife caught him in the act and now he is sliding back in my DMs for a place to crash for the night. It's the audacity for me, but I'm not a saint either in this mess. This is exactly why I called him a Yoruba demon!

Pink Orgasm

My name is Sasha and I have been married to my husband for about 5 years. We went from fucking 3-4 times a week to fucking maybe once in a month. We have had numerous conversations about this and nothing has happened or changed. I wasn't sure if he no longer was attracted to me or had someone else he was involved with outside. He claims he is stressed from work and I just don't buy it. The man I was married to unfortunately wasn't satisfying me and so I had to do something about it.

I had learned about putting an ad out for some dick at a game night a friend invited me to. The lady basically put a paid ad on this site for a man to come over and dick her down. After the game night,

I decided to give it a try even though I was extreme-
ly scared of being killed or beaten up. Unfortunate-
ly because I was so horny I decided to proceed. It
was bad enough that during my break times at the
office I would pull out my dildo and fuck myself in
my office. I first viewed other ads on the website
and saw people posting photos of their private parts
and asking for wild things. I was shook by what I
read but also turned on.

My ad looked like this -

Pink pussy seeking a large dick

Hello! My husband is out of town and I need to be
fucked badly. I need someone to walk in, drop their

*pants and get to work. The door will be unlocked
and the house address is 121 Woodberry JuiceRoad,
Sapphire, IL 10191. Feel free to rough handle me
and the safe word would be "break time". I'm
open to all ethnicities as long as you're bringing a
large thick. Please do no waste my time, as you
walk in there will be a face mask and condoms by
the door. Please wear it before you proceed to enter
further. Hours of operation will be 8pm to 1am.
Thanks*

I had put this ad out on Friday night and got ready
to be fucked. You see, the face mask was to make
sure I didn't remember anyone or feel like the per-
son wasn't attractive enough. It was the mask the
armed robbers usually wore to rob banks that had
holes for their eyes, mouth and usually was a black
color. 8pm came and no one was walking in. I ac-

tually was getting sleepy and heard the door open from my bedroom around 11pm, immediately I turned over and positioned my self in a doggy position with back arched and ass in the air. My heart was beating with fear my pussy was hungry. I heard this person's foots steps get closer and all I heard from the back was his belt unbuckling and him unzipping. I then wiggled my butt a little as I waited for him to insert his manhood into me. I then heard him spitting and the saliva landed on my hole. He then used his fingers to spread his saliva from my butthole to my vagina.

He slid into my pussy and I had an immediate body shock because he was thick down there. I was scared of the size but I also was excited to get my pussy punished. This unknown man fucked my pussy so hard like I was the only woman on earth

226

and he had been awaiting pussy for years. I say this because he was fucking so hard, so fast and I felt drops of his sweat hitting my back. He introduced me to new things as he put my toes in his mouth as he was fucking my pussy. I was feeling so tingly inside, it was a feeling I couldn't explain. He fucked me so hard that I squirted like a fountain and I was very surprised.

Just when I thought he had enough, he switched from my pussy and fucked my butthole. He then pro -ceeded to put his enormous dick into my asshole while he gripped on each side of my butt cheeks. My husband had never fucked me through my ass as he felt it was disrespectful to me, so he always refused to do it when I asked. The last time I got fucked in the butt was in college and I was walking funny the next day. Even though I had this on my mind, I never stopped him or used the safe word. It did hurt and when I tried to push him back, he hit my hand and pushed my back down so i could arch even more than I was before. I allowed him to proceed with his manhood all up in my pink pussy. He went from mild to wild and was pounding my hole like I stole something. I felt every inch in my tum my poking my second wall and I could hear this gushy type of noise from the juice being produced in my hole.

One thing I forgot to add to my ad was to tell the guys to close the door behind them because when I was flipped over I noticed someone else sitting down stroking his dick watching us fuck. He also was using a gavel to hit his balls, this was weird to me like some s&m shit. I wanted to explore new

228

things but this was a little beyond me, unfortunately it was too late to turn back.When the first guy finished he removed the condom and nutted on my titties. I thought the other guy would just watch him bust his nut and walk out but he took off his clothes and D in closer to me. The first was making his way out and the second guy was already in my pussy which didn't even have enough time to take a break. I could have used my safe word but this dick in me had skills and experience it seemed.

His stroked me in ways I couldn't explain and all I could just do was moan aloud to give him the feed back he deserved to hear. He often pulled out in be-
-tween to admire my hole. This man made me work for this pleasure as he flipped me over from doggie to missionary and had me ride him as well. He fucked me so good that I was willing to go the extra

229

mile for him. He pulled out his dick and I knew it was about that time as he stroked his dick and squeezed my mouth open forcefully. He nutted in my mouth and I was still trying my best not to swallow. I could see him smile from the mouth hole on the mask and he gave me a gentle slap on my cheek area and said "good girl". Till today, I haven't told my husband or anyone about this session until now.

I still didn't know any of the men under the masks; it could have been a coworker, my husband's boss or a neighbor I just don't know. I however have no regrets about that night, and while my husband lays near me at night, I rub on my pussy in remembrance.

Thank you so much for being open to reading this book. I hope you find the information in this book helpful.

You can view more of my work on my website at www.BiodunAbudu.com

Feel free to write me at info@biodunabudu.com

Acknowledgments

A special thanks to the following people:

Katherine Knott

South Salatan

You both made this book possible!

ABOUT THE AUTHOR

Biodun Abudu was born in Rhode Island, but comes from a Nigerian background. He wrote his first title, "Tales of My Skin", based on a true life story in 2011. He then released his second title "Stolen Sanity", in 2019, which is also based on a true life story. His third book, "Forbidden Scriptures", was released in 2020. When he is not writing, he works as an artist. In 2011, he graduated with an A.S. degree in Fashion Design, and a B.A. in Merchandising Management with an emphasis on Fashion Merchandising. He currently resides in New York City.

Email : info@biodunabudu.com

Website : www.BiodunAbudu.com

www.ingramcontent.com/pod-product-compliance
Lightning Source LLC
Chambersburg PA
CBHW050415260626
47156CB00003B/1022